GONE
A HUNDRED
MILES

Gone
a Hundred
Miles

Heather Ross Miller

HARCOURT, BRACE
& WORLD, INC.
NEW YORK

for my son,

KIRK
ALEXANDER
MILLER

Everything in this book is entirely fictitious. A portion of the original inspiration was drawn from the diary of Dr. Franz J. Kron. The diary begins 14 November 1835 and ends 8 December 1835. Horticultural information was drawn from Dr. Kron's notes, which begin 19 February 1843 and extend through 8 March 1882. These notes and the diary are there for anyone to read in the Stanly County Public Library, Albemarle, North Carolina.

Heather Ross Miller
July 1967

AN OWL

The pine forest through which he rode was doomed. Sour-
woods crowded it. Also there were yellow poplars, oaks,
and gums, all crowding hard, their roots taking hold in the
grey slate and the sedge. They dropped leaves and seeds
that would obliterate the pines and climax in a hard forest
of a hundred years.

Doctor Tscharner rode on. His black cape brushed the
pines, sending a shower to the dead straw on the ground.
Long fingers of the sourwood shivered in the wind of his
passing. The horse's hoofs struck like hard steel. A white
mist exuded from caves and rock fissures, bellying the

streams that snaked down the sides of the mountain to the river. And the river itself was concealed many miles away. Pieces of slate splintered under the hard galloping horse. They fell over the embankments and sank in the dim water, disturbing snails, the crayfish.

In the tops of high pines, where the limbs thickened and formed craggy arms, an owl dug his talons into the bark. Resin appeared like thin yellow beads. Mist drifted around the owl. He sat listening to the creeping of mice in the leaves below him. His wide-set eyes could not revolve. His head revolved, carrying the locked eyes with it staring straight as the neck turned. He listened, dizzied, perplexed, and, hearing one at a hundred yards, swooped down from the tree and attacked.

The mist came apart and revealed the black horse rearing. The man beat with his fist, clutching always with one hand at the reins, beating and swearing in German. The heavy bird disappeared, was swallowed alive in the rolling white mist. Doctor Tscharner dismounted; the image of the bird still fomented in his brain.

"What madness," he said, stooping to examine the animal. There were long bleeding wounds along the horse's leg. "What madness," he repeated, and slapped his hand against his knee in angry amazement. Such mistakes were unnatural and he knew it. "An owl would not do this," he pointed out to himself. He spoke aloud, alone in the white shrouded forest, with the horse nudging his shoulder.

The galloping legs of the horse could have appeared to have been a small black running thing. "Perhaps. Ah, no. It is unnatural. An owl would never do this. Unless, of course, it was diseased, mad." Doctor Tscharner hesitated in his analysis. The mist rolled over the surface of the streams and they seemed to be steaming. He walked along the embankment and saw that he was in a slate bed. The streams ran through it. The floor of the forest was cluttered with outcroppings where the slate stuck through and exposed itself. Plantain thrived. He broke off the broad leaves and bruised them in his palm. The mystery of the owl annoyed him. He shook his head and, returning to the horse, pressed the bruised plantain to the wounds. He took an ointment of gum from the saddlebags. The wounds were not deep and the blood began to seal them under the plantain juice and the sticky ointment. The horse did not resist him. Doctor Tscharner rubbed the gum and blood from his fingers with a piece of lint and pressed that to the leg. The wounds were not bad. But he decided to walk.

They continued through the pine forest. The man led with the reins drooped over his shoulder. The reins were wet and his cape was wet and both grew more damp as they progressed into the white unsullied mist. They were two black figures, Doctor Tscharner and his wounded horse.

They walked until the mist lifted. The steep path forked down to a meadow of heavy tangling grass. The sun had risen and shone down from a cloudless sky over the cottage. Tscharner paused at the edge of the forest and gazed below. The smoke from the chimney rose in a steady blue column, detaching itself from the broken stones and decayed cedar shingles. A rail fence was falling down and rotting and in many places banks of healthy honeysuckle burst through the rails.

He gritted his teeth and remarked again, "What madness." The earth was red and good, but they only scratched at it. In his homeland, the people cultivated the earth and drew from it all there was to be had with rain and sun and good attention. There the cabbages were raised up so close together you could not set your foot between them, yet there was no crowding. Each cabbage came up perfect, convinced of its place in the soil, the closed leaves tight and green with health. Doctor Tscharner gazed at the tangled meadow with its ruined rail fence. "It is a pity," he said. He shook his head sternly in reproof. There could be no pity. He saw many decayed meadows and as many decayed, ill-repaired, and uncultivated people. He could not pity them.

An old woman came out and stood in the yard, peering up at the mountain, her hand along her eyes. She had sent for him. She had sent a loutish, unwieldy son to tell him of her husband's suffering. The old man's leg was rotting. The son did not offer to return with Doctor Tscharner. It did not matter. The old woman peered intently. Her eyes were poor, but she picked him out and took a handkerchief from her apron and fluttered it in the air. He went down, still leading the black wounded horse.

"I seen you standing up there," she said when he got to her. He said nothing, but led the horse under the stable that was built onto the side of the cottage. She eyed the leg of the horse, the lint that stuck on the bloody and waxy wounds, but she did not remark on them. The doctor was not a talkative sort and his harsh broken speech was hard to interpret. He made himself understood in a thousand subtle ways. His verbalizations, guttural and unnatural, interspersed with German, made him all the more mystifying.

6

She wiped off her face with the handkerchief and took him inside.

The smell of gangrene was infused with the smell of potatoes boiling and the smell of peeled onions. The old man lay on a cot. Doctor Tscharner held up the quilt. Someone had laid bread poultice to his leg. The ragged edges were sprouting blue, blackish dots. They spread as soft and delicate as a fluff of cotton over the putrid flesh.

"Why have you not put a fresh poultice here?" he asked, dropping the quilt.

The old woman peered around him. She sniffed and replied sullenly, " 'Cause. 'Cause fresh bread, clean bread, ain't got any powers of healing." Muttering something more, she went over to the girl who was peeling the onions. "Any idjit knows it's got to be moldy," she whispered, and together they marveled.

He resented the whispering at his back and said sharply, "Say what you like, but this poultice has no power of healing. It has not checked the putrefaction. He may well lose the limb."

The old woman threw down the bunches of onions she had been washing. The bowl clattered on the table and spilled over. A child that he had not seen before began to wail. The girl went quickly to it.

"What you saying?" cried the old woman. Alarm rose in her eyes.

"If I had been summoned earlier, if you had been cleaner, perhaps it would have been more cheerful. But now the mortification has set in and it may be utterly useless. You may as well expect the worst."

"Naw." She ran and grabbed him by the shoulders, turning him around roughly, forcing him to look at her. "Naw. You been summoned and now you here. There ain't nobody in this house can do nothing. That boy of mine ain't fit to kill. He can't even draw water properly. Ain't nobody in this house can do nothing but him, Old Pa." She gestured toward the old man.

Doctor Tscharner stood up. With his feet firmly on the hard clay of the cottage floor, he loomed over her. The odor of onions slid up between them from her red hands clamped on his shoulders. He fixed his gaze upon her, as intense and coldly honest as a beam of light from the sun, and he replied, "I will do what I know and that is all I can do."

He detached each of her hands, slowly, as in a ritual, a shedding off of dead skin. "Yeh," she agreed. "Yeh, I know." Her tone changed and she became old again. She did not resist him.

"It may take all the rest of the day," he said. "I shall try to arrest the spread of the mortification. We must begin at once." She nodded. The girl came back with the child in her arms. Tscharner noticed that its cheeks were unusually red and its eyelids drawn, but he said nothing. He began to instruct the old woman to make a powder of charcoal.

"Put the lumps into the fire twice. When they are red hot the second time, remove them and blow off the ash and pound them. Take care to put them in a dry pot and keep them dry."

He bathed the old man's face and gave him niter dissolved in wine. The mortification was terrible. The old man knew nothing that went on about him. Doctor Tscharner began to apply a blister over the bad flesh, a blistering plaster of linseed, then he took the charcoal powder which the old woman had prepared and dressed the leg.

"Now," he directed her, "we must wait for three hours." He washed his hands in the bowl she had brought for him. "I shall wait outside with the horse."

He walked in the yard. He crossed the wide meadow and examined the fence. The rails were grey-colored, washed by the weather, smooth and enfeebled. The smell of the honeysuckle refreshed him. The loud shrieking of insects in the thick grass drove away the melodrama of the cottage. Doctor Tscharner despised weakness. And he despised his pity and his disgust. He did not have to remain here, waiting on the actions of the charcoal and the linseed to tell him whether or not the old man would lose his leg and perhaps also his life. He could leave it to the old woman to peel away the cataclysm and wash the gangrene off the good flesh. If there was good flesh beneath. He did not have to wait. There were others, wild, half dead, scattered through these mountains. And they all waited on him to come and exchange their bodies. They were clinging to the sides of the planet, scratching at the rich dirt, getting out of it a few potatoes, an acre of corn to throw to their animals that rooted and wallowed and cropped the same rich dirt. He knew the bodies of all. He could ride through their valleys, the meadows choked with brambles, cross over the swift narrow river, ride and ride, riding until one day was absorbed by the next, all of it absorbing, dissolving, obliterating what came before. It was not necessary that he stay here for one old man with a rotting leg.

Doctor Tscharner returned to his horse. The bleeding had stopped. The wounds made by the owl were closed like lips. He smeared more gum on them and threw away the soiled lint. He waited all morning in the meadow. The sun grew warmer and he moved into the shade of one huge oak that cast its wide branches over the exact middle of the meadow. It was the only tree in the expanse of grass and the grass that grew under it was sparse and dry as paper. Its roots rose up out of the earth, convoluted into grotesque shapes, some as high as his knee. He sat down between them and leaned his head against the trunk.

He woke with a start, annoyed with himself for falling asleep, dismayed that he could lose control so easily. It was noon and the girl had brought him a bowl of potatoes. When he finished, he went to the cottage and began to separate the gangrenous flesh. It parted at the press of his fingers. It was the softest black, brownish, sometimes falling pellucid and yellow. The old man knew nothing and did not cry. His stagnant blood collected along the blade of the lancet. Doctor Tscharner took away all that would come and dressed the wound afresh in charcoal and yeast. The smell was very strong. The old woman carried away the morbid flesh. The girl sat nursing her child. He marveled at how she could bear it all, the sight of the wound, the smells, at how she could sit there and calmly offer her breast to the child.

He went back outside. The afternoon passed and in the evening he took away more of the gangrene. The old man seemed to rally. His fingers twitched and he opened his eyes and looked at them. The old woman did not restrain herself. "Lookit, lookit!" Her voice cracked and she burst into tears. Doctor Tscharner felt the skin on his neck prickle. He washed the old blood from his steel lancet.

"He needs tonic and wine. A gill of brandy with gentian." The old woman nodded, unable to conceal her relief. "You will stay the night?" she asked, a wheedling look to her eyes.

"Yes," he replied. "If the gangrene has stopped by morning, there will be no more threat." He ate a supper of cold bread. The girl brewed coffee and poured it for him. The child had begun to cry again and the girl was very agitated. She twisted her hands and tried to speak, but her clumsiness made her bashful. "What is it?" He swallowed the coffee. "What do you need?"

"My youngun is awful fretted," she said. "He been fretted over a day or two. And now he acts like he's trying to stand on his ear. I wisht you'd see to him now that Old Pa is resting." She blushed deeply and twisted her hands as though they were garments full of water.

He went to the child and saw that it was in a febrile state, raising its body up on one side, then crumpling. It was exactly as she had described. The baby appeared to be trying to stand on his ear. Doctor Tscharner turned him over and pressed his fingers to the neck, behind the ear. The child's breathing and rapid pulse indicated summer cold, and this would occasion an earache. Doctor Tscharner peered into the ear. It was inflamed. The child struggled away, shrieking. The girl stood by with her hands hanging limp and stupid down each side of her apron. The fire sputtered and the kettles hissed like acid. The old man groaned on his cot. The old woman had come back and now sat by

11

the fire like a cat, closing her eyes and then opening them. The shrieking of the child did not disturb her.

Doctor Tscharner took his pipe, filled it, and went to the fire. He ignited a splinter of kindling and lit the pipe from it. Drawing a deep breath, he bent over the child and exhaled into its ear. He drew breath again and exhaled in the same way, slowly, cupping his hands around the inflamed ear, squinting his eyes against the smoke. The child became momentarily quiet, his eyelids blinking, his arms and legs, which had been drawn up, sinking, unloosening. The girl whistled softly under her breath. "He's heshed," she said, pleased.

"Yes," said the doctor, "but not for long, I can assure you. There is no doubt an abscess within and the pain will not abate until it has broken. I cannot remove it." He stood up and pointed to the bunches of onions still lying on the table. "Roast some onions for a poultice. Lay it on as warm as the child can bear and bind it in a piece of cloth."

Suddenly the propinquity of them was fatiguing. Their existence in his existence seemed an unbearable intrusion. Doctor Tscharner went out to the flimsy stable. Through the cracks in the wall, which was also the wall of the cottage, he saw them all in the yellow light of the fire. The old woman looked peaceful and feline, contented. Her ugly face was blurred. The girl had begun to peel the onions. The child and the old man were obscure.

The straw in the stable smelled of must. It was old and unclean. He took his blankets and went into the meadow and lay down under the oak tree. The mountains were filled up with black shadows and the leaves of the tree rustled.

Stars appeared. And the wide sky seemed a great black hollow thing, curving inward at the farthest edges.

He fell asleep without thinking of it. Over the narrow flashing river, confined in the forest that covered the mountain, an owl hunted. Doctor Tscharner slept and did not dream of the insane owl that attacked out of pouring mist. He slept with no thoughts. And so slept the old man, his patient, in the smelly, disheveled cottage. And the child slept, a poultice of roasted onions behind his ear. And his mother, the girl, and his grandmother, the old cat, both slept soundly, their mouths opened, snoring barbarously.

In the morning, the gangrene had gone away and bits of good flesh appeared to have been strengthened. The child's ear was still inflamed and he howled with pain. Tscharner gave the girl a small vial of laudanum to put in the ear. "A few drops with warmed milk," he said. "When the abscess breaks, make sure that you wash the ear."

She nodded and unstoppered the laudanum and sniffed it. He stared coldly at her and knew she would not heed his direction. She would not wash the child's ear and it would become infected all over again, would ulcerate, and destroy the membrane, and the child would grow up deafened. He started to scold her, then turned his horse around and rode away. It would do no good. The people did as they liked. They did as they liked and he lanced the boils and drew off the blood. They did as they liked.

He rode back over the mountain. He had collected nothing.

He was intercepted on the river road by a boy belonging to the ferryman Keith. His sister, it seemed, had fallen backward off the yard rail and broken her arm. Doctor Tscharner was to come at once. The boy was not alarmed and stood picking his nose and squinting up through the sunlight at the big man on the bigger horse.

Doctor Tscharner turned toward the river, his bombazine cape billowing. He rode to the ferry landing-place, dismounted, and went into the house. The child lay bawling on a pallet that covered her bed. The others crowded in the door. They were all boys, all dirty, indiscriminately picking their noses like the one on the road, some of them crying like their sister. The fat garrulous wife of the ferryman offered Doctor Tscharner her diagnoses and her explanations. The child, she said, had no business falling and breaking her arm. Her husband, she said, had passengers, or he would have come himself and brought the child to Doctor Tscharner. For ten cents, he ferried people across the river and set them on the opposite side. He could not lose his trade for a girl who had no more good sense than to fall off a fence backward. Already he was half across the Council River, laughing and telling funny stories to his passengers, three men with a wagon. The sounds of the men and the creaking of the ferry cable wimpled through the air.

Doctor Tscharner ignored her. He examined the injury. It was green, the bone bent but in no danger of splintering. The woman's talk was morbid. It infected the child. The others in the door giggled, whimpered, picked their noses, relieved their bowels of gas. The doctor turned and with his harsh, attacking foreign words chastised all of them. They became quiet, eyes bulging, waiting for more.

"Quickly," he commanded, "bring me the cleanest rags,

swathes, anything to be had in this house. And would you possess somewhere either a pasteboard box or perhaps some newspaper?" The woman nodded. "Then fetch me that, also, and the whites of four eggs."

She stood a moment, stammering, then barked down at the child, "Shut your mouth, Cassie." And she moved off. She stopped again at the door. "You want them whites beat?" she asked.

"No," he replied, "but pray bring them in something that is clean." His voice made her feel dirtier than she was and she gritted her teeth until they squeaked.

Doctor Tscharner remained standing, observing the child on the bed. She lay flat on her back, bawling, gulping up great gusts of air. The tears left shiny snail-streaks across her face. She was thin as a bean-stick. He had reached around her arm with his thumb and the end of his middle finger. Her dull brown hair, spreading wild and dusty, gave off a fetid smell, the smell of an unwashed body, the rusty mineral smell of the river. She was perhaps twelve years old. She disgusted him.

She stopped. "You ain't going to bleed me?" She retched on her question. He made no reply but remained standing and staring at her, transfixed, without compassion. He was not fond of children. Neither did he dislike them. He kept a noncommittal dignity and worked to keep it.

Only one time, since arriving in this new land, had he allowed his feeling to intrude. And that one time was painful to his memory. The sight of this child's hysterics and the blathering of her mother recalled it.

It was in Weymouth County, across the river. The child had suffered a long and tedious illness and had been much indulged by his parents and nurses. The parents were wealthy and had entertained many doctors, all of whom had indulged them in their indulgence of the child. Doctor Tscharner's abrupt manner was a diversion. He took them unawares, turning all from the room except two women. He insisted upon topical bleeding as a relief to the boy's fever. He moistened the skin with milk and prepared to introduce leeches to the child's arm. But the very sight of them threw the child into a violent convulsion and alarmed the two women to such a degree that the process was brought to a disagreeable conclusion.

Although he was given a fine and comfortable room in which to spend the night, he knew himself to be insulted. In the morning, the unpleasantness was gone and the boy's ailment had grown worse. But he arose and departed, refusing to continue his treatment.

He chastised himself again, as he had done so often, looking for a refinement, a pressing out of emotion. He had chosen the leeches instead of the lancet. The animals had seemed to him safer for a child than the steel. But it was the sight of them that had caused the panic. He rebuked himself. He should have returned and abruptly and coldly applied the leeches and contained them firmly under a wine-glass pressed on the skin. He should have remained until the treatment was finished. Should not have been toppled by the convulsing child. Should not have been vulnerable to the wounding realization that in the eyes of that child he was hateful and horrible.

He thought of his own child, two years old, plump and short with a blond Dutch bob; his child who had never been ill or injured a day of her life. His heart did not swell with

16

love at the thought of her. But the thought was nevertheless reassuring. He called up every aspect of her body and critically pondered each one, searching for flaws. There were none. Her healthy limbs absolved him.

He returned to the task at hand. He would not bleed this child or any other. His cold reflective silence had chilled her crying to hoarse intermittent sobs. She lay on the pallet and stared at him. Her brothers watched.

"Here." The woman lumbered into the room bearing an apronful of torn strips. A boy followed behind, carrying a newspaper and the egg whites that had been broken and separated into a tin dish.

Doctor Tscharner glowered at them. "I shall need your assistance," he said. She agreed, mopping at the sweat on her neck. "Lay the arm gently on a pillow." She did. He took the grey newspaper and whacked it against his thigh to shake off the dust, then smoothed it and rolled it to fit the child's arm. He slipped it around and his long fingers explored the injured parts, gently pressing and shaping. Then he moistened the torn cloths in the egg whites and began wrapping them around the newspaper splint. With each repetition, he bound firmer, always shaping and pressing the paper and its bandages to fit her arm. When he had set the splint to his satisfaction, he took powdered resin from his saddlebags and sprinkled it over the bandages and continued to wind more on top, dipping each one in the whites and rolling it firmly, interspersing the resin.

He finished and stood up. The room was cloudy with heat. The woman watched him. "You through?"

"Yes," he said. "The splint is good. Lay it always between two pillows. And should she arise, make sure the arm

17

is supported by a sling around her neck, always raising the palm of the hand to her breast."

He gathered his saddlebags, threw on his bombazine, and without another look at the child went down the dusty, foot-tracked hall. As he passed the crowd of brothers, he heard one of them say, "Ain't he going to bleed 'er?" "Naw," answered his brother. "Oh," the first one complained, "I thought to see him bleed 'er."

The bloodthirstiness of the children amused Doctor Tscharner. He crossed the porch. "Don't tamper with my splint," he threatened over his shoulder to the woman waddling in his wake. "Keep the child quiet. Let her eat as she likes. If her shoulder should ache, apply a poultice of stale beer, or vinegar, maybe oatmeal with a little oil warmed. Should her pain persist, perhaps a few drops, perhaps ten, of laudanum would not be unwise. I shall leave it to you."

He said it with cold strength. He fastened the cape around his neck and, before riding off, bent low and said sternly to the ferryman's woman, "I shall expect one dollar and one half for this. If you tamper with my splint, I shall expect to reset the arm and shall ask more money for my trouble." And while she stood enraged and goggling in the sun, he whirled around and was gone.

It was uncommonly warm for early June. The bombazine fell heavy. He urged the horse upward, back onto the road that rose and skirted the Council River, leaving Keith's ferry below. The ferryboat had begun to drift back across toward Larkin County. The children had run out from the house and were straggling down to the banks of the river.

Dust sprang up at his approach. It clouded the underbrush. He urged the horse, but he did not gallop, remembering the owl and the bleeding scratches. They reached the forest. They entered. In the green seclusion, he felt cooled, forgiven. Cooled from the heat of the sudden flaring June. And forgiven for his morbidity. "You are impressionable," he addressed himself. "Impressionable. And that is not safe. Indeed, Doctor, you can hardly call your life your own. Dented and marked, shaped, molded, trod upon, *bruised!*" He shouted aloud, then grew ashamed at his dissimulation. He despised hypocrites. But it was to his advantage and to the advantage of those he treated to exchange his virtues, to replace his wavering feeling of pity and compassion with the preserving realities, often harsh, often cold, frequently absurd. Thus, he was uneasy and angry to discover his cape of practical truth could be torn off by the sight of one crying child, the ignorance of one girl-mother. One must draw down lines and measure off boundaries, seal each seam in the armor. One must murder as skillfully as one must save and deliver. "I am no false man," Tscharner declared.

The horse faltered.

"Easy," he murmured, and cursed the deplorable road. He pulled up and removed the bombazine. His hair was moist and he felt the heat under his eyes and across his lip. He got down and began to lead the horse once more, this time through the noonday forest, where everything was clearly defined and marked, passing through areas of deep green patched in spots of brilliant yellow. He traveled the Kelly Star Road. This road followed the bed of a mountain creek, often covered in brier bushes, confused through narrow gaps, incoherent with stones, strewn about like madness. It lay straight for perhaps a mile, then dissolved into the thickets and did not appear reasonably for two miles.

Doctor Tscharner walked and led the black horse. Sometimes the layers of red dust were peppered in fragments of flint. In bad weather, the people would lay wooden poles crosswise in the mud. And then these would break and shatter under the hoofs of horses. Doctor Tscharner knew. He did not condemn. He matter-of-factly cursed and continued on his way. Here he was, by virtual choice, Doctor Tscharner, black-caped German, riding the mountain all hours. Here he was. He knew the perimeters of his situation and he felt it utterly useless to condemn. So he would ride and curse, appear out of the night or the early morning, appear and lay on his hand, then withdraw whence he had come.

The Kelly Star Road suddenly straightened and opened long out of the forest, banked in yellowish grass and clumps of wild flowers, horsemint and oxeye daisies, small trembling Deptfords, coated in dust, swarming with insects. The Council River was far behind him. The creak of the ferry had been dissipated in the trilling of a thousand wild and savage birds. He walked faster, then, thinking the horse ready, mounted and rode. Apion Mountain lay ahead like an inverted teacup, a modest swelling of earth, too big to be a hill. In its deep forest, the owl slept, his tufted head tucked down, his great tearing beak silent.

2

The wife of Philip Tscharner waited on Apion Mountain. She was not German, but French, having been born in the city of Pouvier, which stood on the River Loire, a river that rose in Massif Central and ran through France like a strand of quicksilver to empty into the Bay of Biscay. She had been born and christened in the tradition of the family Pons as Jeanne-Catherine. In her maidenhood, she wanted nothing from life but to be young and beautiful, a prism of virginity, unstained. Philip Tscharner, the German, came one summer to visit her brother Henry Pons, a fellow student from the College of Delsis in Paris. Philip Tscharner, dark

as night, a prism of steel, with long slender fingers unde-
filed, the fingers of healing, married her. And he brought
her then from the city of Pouvier to America to dwell in a
severe wilderness whose light could not be broken through
a crystal.

He did not call her Jeannette, as she had been called in
Pouvier, but Kaethe. She consented to this change as she
had consented to others. She found herself still young, still
beautiful, but refracting a strange light. From her husband,
Philip Tscharner, she wanted more than he could give. He
possessed education. His movements were those of skill. He
wasted nothing. And he was kind to her. In short, he was a
gentleman and, as such, a genuine rarity in these rude
parts. As for herself, she was clothed, she was well fed,
and, for her amusement, the best of journals, both French
and American, arrived at her home, delivered by the cal-
lused hands of the postboy.

But a kind of paralyzing and ruthless temperament had
begun to spread through her. Doctor Tscharner washed his
hands and washed his lancet, let open the blood of his patients, then washed his hands again and sealed up their
wounds. She waited on the mountain. He was riding away,
always riding away astride the black horse. Gone.

The house grew dark and the slaves brought light. Her
daughter cried and she nursed her back to sleep and laid
her in the crib. The child woke and cried again. Kaethe
took her and lay down with her on the bed of Philip
Tscharner. They fell asleep. The sound of hoofbeats came
in the distance, striking flint into sparks along the Kelly
Star. Doctor Tscharner came into the house. He did not

wish to disturb his sleeping wife. He went out again and slept in the surgery.

Her life was episodic. It had always been that way, happening in isolated incidences without much linking in between. Everything depended on those around her, on those more important. Now everything depended on Philip. And for this, she envied and often resented him in the new wilderness. He said to her that he had been born under a wandering star. He was pleased with that phrase and repeated it and wrote it down in his log. It was perhaps true.

He had come from Jutta in Hesse, the son of a music teacher, the eldest of eleven children. He was perhaps fifteen years old then, having finished the college of Jutta, unrequited, his sharp mind tantalized for more. Paris gave him many opportunities. The libraries, the public lectures, the streets and shops: he found himself in all of them. Medicine drew him to the College of Delsis with its surgery and museums and elaborate botanical garden. All that he saw was pleasing to him, to his temperament, and he was fascinated by the skills of his instructors: Daru, Julien Bavier, Coindreau, and one humpbacked Dutchman called Sechlar. He employed his fingers to grasp the lancet properly, to tie off the ligatures, to distill medicines and roll the pestle.

Curiosity infected him. After finishing his studies at Delsis, he desired to see more of the world. So from Paris he traveled to the south of France, to Bordeaux the seaport, the region of sauternes and clarets; then along the Loire to Lyon in the province of Bourgogne, abundant in more wines, both white and red. He went to Marseille on the Gulf of Lion, then through the provinces of Languedoc and Auvergne, to the city of Limoges, through Poitou, along the twisting Loire again. After the province of Bretagne, he came back up the Loire to the city of Pouvier.

He came to Pouvier in the early summer of 1824 at the request of his friend Henry Pons. They walked along the river, deep in their discussions and arguments. The air they walked through was greenish and redolent. Green leaves floated on the river. An old man scolded a boy for losing a fish.

Doctor Tscharner had plans to travel through Spain, to go to the Netherlands and to Denmark. He spoke of them to his friend. Then he saw the sister called Jeannette. And he was attracted. He learned of her uncle who lived in America, an old bachelor who had made his fortune in gold-mining and who in his dotage had expressed a strong desire to have this niece traverse the ocean and dwell with him. They all talked of it, of the wonders of the new land, of Jacques Pons's wealth, and of his dearth of heirs in that land. Doctor Tscharner became infected anew.

His friend Henry seemed to encourage him, to applaud his infection. The girl had a high proud chin and her hair was an ashen yellow, the color of vermouth. He did not know if he loved her. He felt that he wanted to love her. All her traits appealed to his own. She was abstemious. She did not chatter like her aunts and widowed mother. She could read and thus appreciated learning. She conducted herself in quiet deportment. He could see no reason why they would not be happy. It was wise to make a good marriage.

They were married in July and departed France for America on the first day of September.

She was no longer Jeannette, but Kaethe. She did not trouble herself with this. Marrying Doctor Philip Tscharner was to take her away from Pouvier, the rue St. Etienne. She thought of the riches she was to inherit, of the lands and vast holdings of her uncle. She did not remember him. She could not call up the visage of Uncle Pons. But the excitement of her aunts and mother, the approval of her brother Henry, and the dark elation of Doctor Tscharner shaped her mind. She agreed.

Her virgin nights she had shared a bed with the smallest sister, Cécile. Kaethe's crystal naïveté would not recognize the harsh probability that, while she was away, this small Cécile would grow up and turn old in the same bed under the window, Cécile, who still sucked her thumb and sometimes wet the bedclothes. She would not believe she could be away so long a time.

Away they went. They went aboard a sailing ship at Le Havre. She did not like the sea, its sight or its smell, and the rolling of the vessel gave her a great giddiness to which were added nausea and costiveness. This unpleasantness continued the whole of the voyage, and he could not persuade her to come out on deck and exercise and breathe the fresh air. She lay in the bunk and swallowed teaspoonfuls of ether followed by glasses of water to relieve the convulsions in her stomach. The water seemed to her repulsively brackish, with a bad smell and sediment in the bottom of the glass. He dispensed to her sulphur or magnesia flour. She longed for a stalk of rhubarb.

He grew tired of holding her hand and moistening the cloths for her head. He went on deck and walked and looked at the sails spreading in the wind. He liked it, the wind and the rolling sea and the ship under sail, the hoarse commands of the sailors. He conversed little with the other passengers. The sea occupied his whole attention. It dissolved endlessly into the horizon, streaked with white, glittering under sunlight or moon. When its waves reared twenty feet or more and the captain ordered all below, Doctor Tscharner lay in his bunk and listened to the sounds of the sea thrashing around the flimsy vessel. The sounds of the angry sea both pleased and frightened him. The ship lurched through the waves and Kaethe whimpered and grew more ill. He comforted her, but his mind was more in sympathy with the sea.

They arrived in New York by the last of September and then traveled, again by ship, along the eastern seacoast to the port of Wilmington. There the Cape Fear ran into the Atlantic, adding mud to the grey salt water. Doctor Tscharner and his wife took passage on a barge up the Cape Fear to the city of Fayetteville. The tolling of the barge's bell echoed through the flat sandy woods. At times the river was muddy and at others it gleamed with a peculiar greenish clarity. He saw people, like shadows, come out of the woods and stand on the river bank. Bunches of grey moss hung from the trees.

In the market at Fayetteville, they saw, for the first time in both their lives, Negro slaves. They traveled the rest of their journey in a coach drawn by horses, and by the time they reached Uncle Pons, some two hundred miles in the hills of North Carolina, it was late November.

It was a bad move. Jacques Pons did not expect the German. His plan was to marry this niece to a man of his own choosing, a man he could control and thus control forever the measure of his wealth. He did not expect the tall sharp German.

And Kaethe did not expect the rain. It fell in a miserable grey drizzle, cold and unkind, spotting her clothes. They got down from the coach and found Uncle Pons out at the barn shucking corn with his slaves. His wealth extended over eight thousand acres in Weymouth County, bordering the Council River, encompassing the forests. Added to this were his swine and cattle, his cane, his gold mines, and his brace of slaves. Uncle Pons was rich. But here he sat in the barn and shucked corn with his slaves. He sat in the barn and did not offer them shelter from the November drizzle.

Swarms of gnats flew over the dry shucks and settled on the hard cobs. Pons grasped the corn severely, tore off the shucks, and tossed the cob into a wooden bin. His hands were rough, his nails broken. His niece felt paralyzed, destroyed. She stepped forward into the mud of Weymouth and greeted her uncle bravely, extending her hand. "Are you well, dear Uncle?" she asked.

He got up, brushing the shucks from his pants, and took her hand and pressed it to his lips. "In my prime," he bellowed. "In my goddamned prime." His eyes roved over Philip Tscharner, tall and stern, his eyes set like chips of black glass in his smooth face. "Who is that?" he demanded.

She turned. "My husband. Doctor Philip Tscharner."

Tscharner faced the old man. Their glare was long and intense. They disliked each other. Pons grunted. "Then, into my house, you both." He begrudged them every mouthful, every sheet on their bed, every labor of his slaves to make them comfortable. Doctor Tscharner did not remain long at a time in the house of Jacques Pons. He rode out each day seeking his practice among the people, staying all day, crossing the Council River into Larkin County. The ferryman called Keith took him over and brought him back. Slowly, but assuredly, his influence spread through the people on both sides of the river. They talked about the strange foreign doctor who rode a swift horse, black and well fed. Of the strange dark-eyed doctor who could examine and absolve. He inspired awe among them, a kind of fearful trust.

While he was gone, the house of Pons was strained and uneasy, tugging ruthlessly at the reins of insanity. Kaethe was caught. During the long day, her uncle spat and whispered in her ear against Philip Tscharner, calling him names, assassinating him relentlessly. She hated Uncle Pons, but she could do nothing. She waited all day for Doctor Tscharner's return in the evening, and when he was kept away into the night, it wounded her unbearably.

The winter passed with all its specialized dreariness and she had hardly left the house to see the new land. Summer came and it was so hot she couldn't. The only breezes were hot and dry, quick agitations that disturbed the withering trees and brought no comfort. She had become pregnant. She wished to be away from this place.

The time turned right for Doctor Tscharner. "I wish to go, Pons." He faced the old man with grim courtesy. "I am tired of waiting, enduring your wickedness. You made promises to my wife, in letters to her family. But you have fulfilled nothing. Indeed, I think you shall never." It was night and they stood near the river which rippled in silver-ish bands. Against the smooth waters, his silhouette wavered and spread away into darkness. He spoke evenly, with no emotion, and he used the French of Pons. "Your promises mean nothing to me. I shall take my wife and leave."

The sound of the French was like tinder. The old man sprang into flame. "You, Hessian! Could you not wait until I was in my grave? Have I not kept a roof over your heads, the both of you? And when your brat comes, would he not bawl and puke in my house, making my sheets filthy?" He struggled with the French he had not spoken in years. The words came readily to his mind, but his tongue failed. "Hessian! Son of a bitch! *You* are tired!" He strode off. The water was like a sheet of metal. Doctor Tscharner kept silent. The veins in his neck were hard as cords; his eyes, black stones.

The old man returned. "Go, you may, of your own accord. But I'll not *put* you off. I'll not give *you* that pleasure." He disappeared, making the noises of a dog, huffing, barking at the moon in the river.

"Go, you may!"

He knew exactly where to go. Across the river, forty miles out of Pons's territories, and at least twenty miles more up through hilly forest edging the river in Larkin County. He had bought it on one of the long trips into the forest and kept it secret, ready for his defiance of Pons.

The house stood on a low hill, banked by mountains to the north and south, the most prominent of which was called Apion. The roaring of the Great Falls on the Council could be heard. The house faced the only market road in

Larkin County, the road from Salisbury to Fayetteville which was called the Kelly Star. It was not the place for a rich planter like Jacques Pons. Of precious minerals it had but few. And there was no room for spreading fields. But it was sheltered from the worst of the winter blasts. And he had bought it, the house, the land, and the eight slaves attached to it.

He inspected them carefully, with interest, with a feeling of embarrassment at owning human flesh. In the larger of the two cabins lived Ishmael, a giant black man with arms the size of tree trunks, his wife, Pheny, who kept the kitchen and who was of slight stature, with arthritic swelling in her fingers. And these had three children, two girls, called Lottie and Maud, and a boy, called A. D., all healthy, with clear round eyes that followed his every move. In the smaller cabin were two Negroes, younger than Ishmael and Pheny, a man, Clegg, and his wife, Rutha, who had just been delivered. She lay in bed suckling a boy as yet unnamed.

He looked at them all. The cabins were sound and dry, with a fireplace in each. The slaves looked at him: this foreign white, a proud man, a German, a man who healed by the laying on of hands. They looked at this new master and they were unsure. He spoke to them in low tones, and though his speech was broken by accent, his grammar and manner of language were correct. And this correctly spoken language, to their ears, was suspicious.

He felt he was a scarecrow before them, his black chattels. The situation fascinated and puzzled and truly depressed him. He went out with the man Ishmael and looked at the woods and fields. The trees were excellent, the earth spongy to his foot, and the last master had left him an apple orchard of high quality. The house was not large and had no fine appearance. But it had new shingles and the chimneys drew the smoke cleanly.

Doctor Tscharner set about, determined to make it work for him. The Kelly Star would be profitable for his practice. And the people here had not seen a physician, some of them, in their entire lives. He set about and he was determined.

When he left, he gave Pheny an ointment for her finger joints and ordered warm fomentations. He extracted an abscessed tooth from the jaw of Ishmael's son, A. D., and gave him camphor pills for his pain. He examined the newborn and saw that it was approximately six or seven days old. The navel string had not dropped off and hung by a thin filament of skin which he divided and bound with a soft rag. He admonished his slave Rutha to lie in her bed and avoid flooding.

Doctor Tscharner gathered his medicines and instruments and buckled the saddlebags. He rode away on the big horse and they watched him go, their minds filled with wonderment. Rutha gave her boy a name: Doctor.

And to this house he brought Kaethe, heavy in pregnancy, soon after the middle of July. She looked at the rough logs of the dwelling, papered with newspaper on the inside, harboring nests of wasps. She blinked at the crowding wilderness on every side, the two high mountains, the sound of the distant Falls spiraling through her ears. She stared upward at the raw blue sky over it and then closed her eyes without a word. "Take me down from the wagon," she murmured, "and be easy."

The child was born in August. He examined it with care and curiosity. That it was not a son did not seem to matter now that it was born. It was healthy and large and bawled vigorously. He gave her to the slave Pheny to wash and wrap.

Doctor Tscharner left the house and walked to the mountain creek flowing westward at the foot of the slope. At his approach, the insects stopped, birds flapped away, a serpent faded. He lay down. He listened to the brown iron water bubbling over stones and dead limbs. He lay and listened. The planet turned beneath him and the constellations changed an infinitesimal measure of their positions. He lay by the brown creek and thought of this child which he had fathered. A lot of scarecrows they were becoming. Hessian, French, and now this new one who by chance of the land on which she had been born was to be called American. He was becoming complicated, defiant of analysis, yet at the same time also diluted, spread thin.

Doctor Tscharner wrote in his log that night. There was no breeze to diminish the candle. Moths fluttered.

Hot and fair. Wind from the south all day. Remained home to attend Kaethe. Elisabeth Tscharner born in the forenoon. A fine girl. August 17, 1825.

3

So the wife of Doctor Tscharner, who waited and grew ill
of waiting in the house of her rich uncle, had to wait again
in her own house. She listened to the roar of the Great Falls
and when she had listened to it day in and day out, continu-
ing into the night, she conjured in her mind exactly how it
looked, its foaming whiteness, its high clear spray dashing
over the grey rock, the lichens and the ferns that thrived in
its moisture. She did not go out and seek it to see for herself
and confirm her visions. She remained in the house and was
attended by her slaves. And when she had a daughter to
occupy her hours, she sat by the window and held her. How

completely this child existed nursing at the breast. Kaethe marveled. She marveled at the intense power that rested on the child's faintly twitching eyelids, on its sucking lips, in the soft pulsations of the fontanel. The eyes which opened and looked at her, blank and unwieldy, reflected the image of her own eyes looking down. The child pleased her and she came to love it in the tedious hours. She found herself gathering before it like a swarm of bees to the comb.

But the child grew and then outgrew the breast. The blank and unwieldy blue in her eyes was replaced by flecks of brown, then hard darkness. They did not so much reflect any more, as pierce through and examine. The first things that Lieschen saw as soon as she was able to grasp the window ledge and peer out were trees, rows and rows of endless trees, militant and green. Her fingers slipped. She collapsed in a soft heap. The trees swayed, their leaves quaking; then they stiffened to a thousand green spearheads glistening.

Her mother gathered her up with kisses, chucking her under her fat chin and patting her cheeks. Her mother was a pale-yellow vision, a pair of white hands, a thrusting breast. There were dark hands that took care of her body, the hands of slaves. And there was a pair of different hands that lifted her on occasion and examined her with their long fingers. And to these hands there was another vision, a face with strange black eyes and a black cape swinging. And added to this was a horse, black, galloping.

Thus she was a child of visions, surrounded by particular terrors and comforts, spoken to in a multiplicity of tongues, French and German, slave Gullah, and the halting accented English.

Kaethe held her before the window. June sun broke in a brightness through the thick forest and in the small panes of the window. The glass was imperfect, flawed with bubbles and streaks. It appeared to be melting. Lieschen held out her hands to the glass. Kaethe looked only at the flaws, scrutinizing every streak that took on the color of honey. It was an imperfect glass, made for seeing through, but for seeing through with unreal eyes. Unreal glass, unreal world. This was the world she saw.

She stamped her foot. The braided rug, made of rags, full of color, braided and dyed by her slaves, lay clumsy on the floor. "What fools," she hissed. What innocent and trusting, dew-fed fools they had been. And it had been so easy. That was the most wounding part of it. It had been so easy to talk of wealth and a comfortable posterity when standing in the cosy parlor in Pouvier, Philip poised with a wineglass, her brother Henry, her silly aunts all clustered around her equally silly mother reading Uncle Pons's false letters. "Come," said Jacques. "Come here to me."

And here she was. Such fools they had been to trust. That was the first mistake. She stamped her foot again. It was a gesture she would not tolerate in anyone. She had been born almost nobility, possessing superior qualities, raised up to perpetuate those qualities. They did not include stamping feet or weakening to emotion any more than they did belching. But she had fallen idle. Her superior qualities were ebbing. She put Lieschen down on the rug. Her stormy mood depressed her. She had never known the dimensions of herself until she came here to this mountain. Now she stormed and raged and stamped her foot as rudely as any ill-bred woman. She did not do it before her husband,

Philip Tscharner. Before him, she was still perfect. She was a transparent stone.

Kaethe sighed and turned to the window again. The flawed glass had assumed a familiar meaning to her. Each whorl and cell contained a symbol that she knew how to read. She felt she knew this glass better than she knew his face.

He had ridden away early, eating a sparse breakfast, packing bread in the saddlebags. Patients arrived at the surgery asking after "Doctor Shanner." Ishmael instructed them to leave their names in the daybook if they could write. And if they could not write, they came to the house and asked "Miss Katie" to do it for them. She listened to the names: Mattie Bell, a withered mouth with bad teeth, an ulcer in the gum; Toby Zane, an infant with clubfoot, his mother most desirous of a quick and painless cure; Pearl Blalock, a falling of the fundament, much aggravated by costiveness.

The names blurred into the names of their illnesses and complaints, warts, corns, bleeding at the nose, a baby with thrush on his tongue, his mother's nipples sore and scabbed. She burned to get away, not to have to listen to and smell. She prayed for his return. Whole mornings and afternoons were passed. Sometimes he did return, unexpectedly, galloping up the slope, to her great rescue.

But he did not come in and sit down to hold her hand. He received the patients, took off their clothes, listened. She grew resentful. The smell of the surgery was enough to bring her resentment whether he was there inside it or gone away. The Bunsen flame opened quietly at his touch, blue, like the quiet forked tongue of a snake. The odor of dried

36

foxglove, camphor, blue vitriol annoyed her. He pounded things in the mortar and rolled pills, patiently rolling the grains until they adhered and became solid.

She resented all of this and did not entirely know why. She sat and stared through the window, across the yard at the small log surgery, and wondered at herself. The yard would be pelted with thick grey-colored rain or weighted under a torpid sun. It seemed there could be no days of medium saturation, mild, pallid days of no weather.

She wondered that she could sit there in such a hateful state. He had done nothing to deserve her attitude. The times when he was close to her were worse than those when he was far gone, across the river, the mountains, bleeding, delivering, closing the thin eyelids of someone's death. What difference did it make to her any more? She demanded to know.

Doctor Tscharner was overwhelmed by her resentfulness. It was entirely unrealistic and unorthodox. Sitting at table, herself lovely and cold, glittering in her new frost; himself stiff and hard, bound with iron against the attack of this weather, Kaethe at last forced the issue. She put him to the question. The question of staying on in this place. The question of crossing back.

He put down his fork and stared at her, not truly believing she could ask such a thing. He lifted the wineglass and sniffed. "Is this not my wine?" he asked. She nodded, surprised at his maneuver. "Did it not come from my grapes?" he asked again. "Yes," she said, "but that has nothing to do with what I have asked you."

Doctor Tscharner drained the glass. It was not more

than two ounces. He uncorked the bottle and poured more. "It has everything to do with what you have asked, Kaethe," he corrected her. He absorbed her with a long, quiet, paralyzing stare.

They resumed eating. She tasted her blood in the food she put in her mouth. At the end, she made one more remark, throwing all her dice into it.

"It was a kind of suicide to come here," she said, "to abnegate that other life, those other selves we had." She smiled wistfully, her chin very high, revealing smooth flesh underneath. She picked up the small table bell and rang.

Doctor Tscharner spoke no more of it. But Kaethe could not let it rest. Daily she examined her trap and daily it grew more inescapable. She paced like an animal through the house, pausing before the window to stare at the high blue-firred mountain, at the pine and oak trees that grew nearer, back through the house, out to the kitchen, where Pheny and Rutha stirred, stepping into the yard, a bonnet tied on her head, squinting against the sun.

In the past, it had soothed her to suckle the child. Now the child had teeth and ate stronger stuff than her fluids could provide. She had nothing to succor or to be succored by. He was always riding away. She alarmed herself by wondering if he would come back each time he stayed away over the night. After all, she scolded herself, he could really have no desire to return to her. She was like a fragile piece of furniture, an adornment, with no real function. The slaves ran the house and the farm in his absence, acting on the orders he had left them. She was a figurehead.

Kaethe tormented herself without end. And added to it

was the bitter gall that she would now never return across. Here she had come and here she would stay and watch Lieschen grow up and get her grandchildren, all of whom would be locked in the wilderness. She could not bear to let it rest. She had to try all over again.

She decided to attack. He sat writing in his log. He wrote:

Warm western winds. Scattering clouds. I was called off across the river into Weymouth County. An outbreak of epidemic. River low. No fish. Tomorrow the Sabbath.

She appeared at his elbow. "Oh, Philip," she croaked like a frog, "why not? Why not?" She ran to the bedroom and caught onto one of the bedposts and clung to it crying terribly.

Again she had overwhelmed him. He sat stunned for a moment, then put away the log and the pen. He went to the bedroom and stood watching her. She clung to the post like a child swinging from a tree. The buttons on her basque had come undone and the white of undergarments showed. He waited, forming the right thing to say. Doctor Tscharner got it ready, thoroughly diagnosed, ready to inject with precision where it would cause the least pain and then close up, heal.

"On the wall of the kitchen in Jutta, there was a piece of embroidery sealed in a glass. My mother made it. It said *Kinder, Kirche, Küche.* Do you know what those words mean, Kaethe?" He injected quietly.

She paused, translating, then the understanding came to her face and she was ashamed. Tears glittered. "Yes," she replied, barely moving her lips. He had been easy to her, kind, undemanding of her labor, conscious of her comfort. She was ashamed. She was sorry that he had not beaten her, attacked with scorn and cursed. She wanted to tear off her clothes and be naked.

She searched for a rejoinder. The pieces for the puzzle were scattered. "Philip," she said, "I cannot know your mother. And your father, your sisters and brothers. You so seldom speak of them. I know nothing, Philip." She sank on the bed, her hands covered by her skirt. "You know everything of me," she concluded.

The argument was lost. *Kinder, Kirche, Küche*. She repeated them in her mind. They were the places of women. The motto for any respectable wife, an empress or a peasant. Of children, she had brought forth one, a daughter, and that daughter remained unchristened. Of the kitchen, of the church. She stopped. The words had a dull sound, dead, dull, ironbound. She felt for his hand. "Philip," she murmured, gazing dreamily at his face, "how many times do you suppose your mother pricked her finger and bled?"

Doctor Tscharner did not answer. Kaethe withdrew into sleep. And in her sleep, she examined drops of blood, dried brown. She picked up the embroidery hoop and placed it like a crown on her head.

4

He became obsessed with the need for growing things. He desired every arable inch to be cultivated and prospering at his hand. The lecture books from Delsis were pulled from their niches and thumbed through and marked. Botany, the vascular flora, the magnificence of the plant world impressed him all over again.

The slaves plowed and laid out the rows in drills and raised up his vegetables, many of which were unknown and uneaten in Larkin County. They wondered at his eating the tomato, pulpy and red, shaped like a trophy. It was to them as poisonous as the nightshade.

And his cabbages amazed them. He raised the compact savoy, with its wrinkled leaves stretched tightly around its head, as tight as the membrane on the end of a drum.

The eggplant lay about, its long purple fruits glistening in the gardens. And its cousin, the pekin, was as striped as China silk and equally rare. Both of them suspicious, tantalizing.

The land was manured and opened and manured and broken, spaded by hand, tamped down under the black bare feet of Ishmael and Clegg. Doctor Tscharner gave every spare minute to the land. When he had finished raising and opening the bodies of men, he appraised and treated the land. His notebooks were filled with scribblings about the planting times for Handon lettuces, broccoli, and endive, the multiplication and separation of onions. He was not content with the culture of vegetables. He began to explore the genetics of fruit, the arts of grafting. His fingers became familiar with the feeling. He fitted twigs and shoots into the living plant so that they took hold and became part of it and affected its heirs.

The slaves planted vines and trees for him in every corner of the land, laying out future orchards and gardens, refurbishing the world with fig, sweet almond, Moorepark apricot. Doctor Tscharner grafted plums onto peaches, pears onto apples. The results pleased him and lay in his hand, heavy and ripe, yellow, freckled with pinkness.

He bought three tropical plants and moved them into a small heated shed with a wall of small-paned windows facing south. They were two orange trees and a lemon. The oranges were tagged *Seville*. Of the lemon, he had only the assurance that it was a *Citrus limonia*. Nothing more.

42

Vineyards were raised on the slope of Apion Mountain. He ordered new varieties. He became an epicure of plants, indulging himself, wallowing in the sensuous feeling their produce gave him, their smells and flavors, the sight of them growing.

And the more he knew, the more he became obsessed with the need. He learned from his slaves the times of the first swarm. Clegg was one who could move among bees and not be attacked. His smell did not alarm them. He could come away with hundreds of them crawling over his hands and never suffer a sting.

The bees came out of the woods in a buzzing, teeming throng, surrounding their queen, who sought new lodging. Her departure threatened the life of the swarm. They clung around her. And when she lit on the branch of a tree, they settled around her, their filmy wings working as rapidly as the bubbles in boiling water.

"Watch, now," said Clegg in a whisper.

The bees formed a long buzzing pyramid, very wide and thick at the top, next to the limb where the queen rested. Clegg grinned. "They ready." He slipped up under the tree and held a hive under the pyramid of bees. "Now," he nodded at Ishmael, who was swathed in clothes, his face wrapped like an Arab's. Ishmael gave the limb a shake and all the bees fell into Clegg's hive. He clapped on the lid and listened to the angry buzzing inside. "She's in thar," he assured Ishmael and Doctor Tscharner. "We got the old gal in thar and they ain't going to leave 'er." He grinned at his master.

Doctor Tscharner was pleased. It was an excellent hive and with luck the bees would work excellent combs. The yellow wax he needed for his medicine. And the clear, yellowish honey would sweeten his table.

The bees buzzed violently. "As fierce as a storm of the steppes," he remarked, "a terrible shrieking buran. Of wind and of dust."

Doctor Tscharner sowed the land and made it prosper. He captured the swarming of its bees. He calculated the running of its shad in spring water. On uncommonly warm evenings in February, Pheny would hold up her hands and say, "Listen! Shad frogs hollering." And the trees and undergrowth would seem to explode in the noises of the creatures. Then the next day would be cold and bitter and there would be no shad frogs hollering. But Pheny would repeat herself many times over, "Shad frogs hollering the other evening. Time for river shad soon."

And in March these fish made their way through the rivers to spawn in fresh water. Ishmael and Clegg and the boy A. D. built fish dams on the Council River and trapped basketfuls of shad. Part of the fish were dried and salted, rendered into oil. But the best of them were baked and put on the table. Pheny mashed bits of the white fish in a plate for Lieschen. She rubbed it round and round with her finger, making sure there were no bones, before she put it in the child's mouth. Pheny was slow and took a long time with the shad. Lieschen devoured it as soon as it was put in her mouth. "Lizzie! I declare," grumbled the Negro, "you eats as fast as a guinea. Did you chew that?"

The rarity and wealth of Doctor Tscharner's table took on the scope of his notoriety. Larkin natives came as much to see the curious gardens, and perhaps glean a taste, as to have their ills treated.

Only in the cultivation of flowers was he disappointed. They were ornamental and took up space, edging the rough corners of the house. And they gave the air a sweet smell in their season. But beyond this, they were useless and did not give back the nutrients they took from the land. But he would not let them be moved from their places.

The herbs of the land he desired to know more intimately. But he could not spend his time wandering in the woods and he left herb gathering to the slaves. His life was full. The practice of medicine filled him, the cultivation of the land enriched him. He did not hesitate to take off his cape and join the labor of the slaves. They cut their eyes at him, embarrassed, amused at the master who worked their work. Doctor Tscharner did not notice. He gave attention to the soil, the thrusting forth, the flourishing and increase of his dimension.

And on the Sabbath he rose up and went about his work as always. The sun came clear over the mountain. It shone through the sourwood, the elm and oak and pine, through the sloping river birch. Their roots pierced the moist earth. Their system was complex and assured. On the river, the ferryman took people over and set them on the other side. The wind carried their sounds. There came the faint lapping of water wafting the shout of the ferryman as he approached the shore. Mules pulled the wagons aboard with a dry plodding sound. The gate bumped against the red clay banks and the cables whined. Then there would be a space of no sounds. Then the lapping of the water returned.

Wagons rumbled along the Kelly Star, full of farmers

and their untidy families on the way to a meetinghouse called Rocky Run. The preacher there was known as Lentz and he was not a man of the cloth, invested by the hand of the church. But he was a man of the calling, singled out by the invisible Hand.

With his native congregation, Lentz held a comfortable working arrangement that served both spirit and flesh. They plowed off a few acres on his plot, sat him down to their tables, and he in return heard out their confessions at revival, soused them in the river, and made absolving visitations. He did not like Doctor Tscharner. The doctor made no confessions, displayed no familiar sin, and his uncanny, unpredictable visits among the people held a troubling measure of sanctity. Lentz suspected the foreigner of Catholicism. "A devil from the legions of the Pope, no doubt," he grumbled to his old woman. And she agreed, tightening her lips and tucking in her chin.

Doctor Tscharner did not choose to make his appearances at Rocky Run a habit. The religion that was passed from hand to hand inside the meetinghouse, broken into pieces and devoured, did not attract him. He went there on occasion to satisfy his conscience toward his wife, Kaethe, who he felt needed to join in friendly relations with the *Frauen*.

He rose and shaved himself of the black beard that grew on his long trips away. He put on fresh garments, but no hat. With Kaethe at his side in the wagon and the slave Pheny holding Lieschen in the back, he stiffly approached Rocky Run. He tied the horse to the rail. And they entered the rough meetinghouse made of peeled logs.

The people turned, murmuring, coughing, and then turned back. Doctor Tscharner stood at the end of a bench and allowed his wife to pass before him and take her seat.

A thin man stood up and lined off the first verse of a hymn. He held the only hymnbook in the house. The people stood and listened, fastening on to the words, then they broke into stumbling song. *Jesus, Lover of my soul, Let me to Thy bosom fly, While the nearer waters roll, While the tempest still is high!*

The tongues rolled over the words and the bosoms swelled. The thin man lined off another verse, his nasal tenor voice breaking at the corners. Lentz, the shepherd, stood glowering and singing as badly as the rest.

The baldness of Rocky Run resounded in singing and the immense wilderness surged up to windows that were propped open with sticks of kindling. A stray chicken circled in the yard, pecking at the dust, stretching its neck to incredible heights, clucking irritably. Dirt daubers had built combs of mud in the rafters of Rocky Run. Some of them were old and dry, a faded ashen color; others were new and wet, fresh with a tiny black aperture at the end of each tunnel. *Hide me, O my Saviour, hide, Till the storm of life is past, Safe into the haven guide, O receive my soul at last!*

The singing was finished. They sat down. Lieschen wallowed on Pheny's lap. She peered into the faces of her parents. They stared ahead at some inscrutable image on the wall behind Preacher Lentz. He began to pray, his hands clasped in a big-knuckled knot under his chin. The heads of the people fell forward and their eyes shut. Doctor Tscharner did not bow. Kaethe did not kneel or shut her eyes. Lentz prayed long and heavily, stopping for breath and to clear his throat. He was an old man. He was old and

loud and his face grew crimson as he prayed. Feet dangled
over the hard benches. Eyes cracked open and peeped curiously around. When they saw the stiff unbowed head of
Doctor Tscharner and the smooth chin of his wife, the eyes
snapped shut again and the breath was sucked sharply.

They were astounded. The wives' heads buzzed with the
talk they would make later. There was one who took full
notice and was amused and silently applauded the stern un-
bending temperament of the doctor. This one was the miller Aaron Bloodworth.

When the plate came, Doctor Tscharner laid a large coin
in it. Lentz was indignant. It was gold that came from sickness, from the letting of blood. The German's money carried all sorts of taints. He wanted to refuse it. But when the
plate came back again and he emptied it, he saw that Doctor Tscharner's coin was three-fourths the gain. He kept it.
And at the close of the service, he put out his hand to the
German.

The doctor's grip was hard. His long fingers tightened
over Lentz's cold weak ones. The women in the yard noticed the width of Kaethe's skirts, the whiteness of her face,
the red-stone ring on her hand. "Thatun don't do nary a
thing," they whispered enviously. "Don't look natural, does
she? You think?"

Aaron Bloodworth strolled in the dust, absorbing the
whispers, taking stock of the envy, the uncontrolled open-
mouthed awe. He saw how the doctor fastened his fingers
on Lentz and overwhelmed him with quietness. These
things were pleasurable to Aaron Bloodworth. He approved
of Doctor Tscharner and his peculiarities. He felt replenished by the sight of them.

They drove off. Small bells tinkled in the harness on the horse's back. They drove the long tunnel of river trees and the noon sun fell on them in hot yellow spots. Bloodworth gazed after them until they turned and were absorbed by the trees of the mountain. His wife, Hannah, tugged at his sleeve. "Do you reckon they's Catholics?" she queried. Bloodworth threw back his head and laughed. Hannah listened disapprovingly. She glanced at the people who were looking at his loudness. "Aaron," she said, "hesh yourself." He stopped. Looking at her soberly, he replied, "Naw. Naw. What would a real Catholic step inside of Rocky Run for?"

He burst into laughter again. Hannah disapproved with vigor.

After his meal, Doctor Tscharner retired. Kaethe sat for a while on the porch staring at the mountains. Then she decided to take the child and go to visit one of the *Frauen* who had smiled at her and had been nice. They would go to visit Evalina Tyne, a widow, who lived near the Kelly Star, on the opposite slope of Apion. They would not go far, she assured Pheny, but they would take Maud and Lottie with them.

She tied a white cap on Lieschen. They went down the grassy slope. It was the first lawn ever to be clipped in Larkin County. Ishmael and Clegg and A. D., all down on their knees or bending over the small Dutch sickles, kept Doctor Tscharner's grass shorn down and thick as velvet.

The cut grass gave out a dry pungence. Kaethe sniffed, surprised that she could enjoy such a smell. Lottie and Maud, each leading Lieschen by a hand, found the cleared path in the woods. She followed behind, absently listening to their chatter.

A rustling blew toward her from the willow oaks on the river. The rustling shuttled through her hair, raising it up from the scalp. She put up a hand to smooth the hair and noticed the white clouds in the sky. *Sunday afternoon. Winds and clouds from the southwest. Scattering clouds. Lieschen knows it is Sunday by her dress. Otherwise it is as any other day in the wilderness.* "There," she said to herself, "I put it as aptly as could be put. As well as he."

The river path narrowed, and Kaethe stepped ahead to lead the child herself. The sun was hot and she kept to the shade as best she could, tripping occasionally over roots. They would visit Evalina Tyne in silence, in a quaint polite little ceremony: Evalina making clumsy gestures, offering them things to eat; Kaethe nodding, perhaps smiling and tasting something, then nodding again, folding and unfolding her hands. *Madame Tyne, I cannot speak to you well. This is my daughter, Elisabeth Tscharner. It is wrong, I know, to shut oneself away from friends. Yes, I am wearing a carnelian. It is clear. It is red. It is mine.*

Lieschen had stumbled and was down on her hands and knees in the red dirt. She was crying; the skin of her palms was raw. Tears dropped on her white dress. Red dirt had soiled the hem. Kaethe sat down with the child in her lap. She did not care about the red dirt. She did not care about the slave children who witnessed. She brushed away the tiny stones that were sticking in Lieschen's hands and, like Lieschen, began to cry.

They sat and cried and the sun beat down. She began to cry harder than Lieschen, so much harder that the child

50

stopped and stared at her. "Mama, Mama," she called, looking at the tears on Kaethe. She put her finger on one, then stuck the fingers into her mouth. Then she stopped looking at Kaethe and gazed at the man who had come up behind them. She did not call to him. She sucked her finger and gazed.

Kaethe did not see. Her shoulders shook with the sobs. Her crying was ruthless, coarse, unkempt. The slave children Lottie and Maud were infected by it and began to bleat.

Lieschen stared around at them and, concluding that they had arranged it all for her amusement, took her finger out of her mouth and grinned.

Doctor Tscharner went away. He went the way he had come, his shoulders stern in the air, the sun glinting off his back in a blue-blackish sheen.

5

Doctor Tscharner rode back to see the old man with the gangrenous leg. Good flesh had taken hold. It would live and perpetuate his strength a few more years. The old woman pressed some coins in Doctor Tscharner's hand. They amounted to eighty-nine cents in copper. And she gave him a mess of venison freshly dressed.

He did not see the girl with the baby. "My son carried off his woman and youngun." The old mother shook her head. "It was a lucky blessing you come when you did and saved my old man's leg. I'd of been down and out without nary a one here." She smiled at Doctor Tscharner and gestured toward the venison. "I shot that deer my own self."

He returned to the ferryman's child. He removed the splint. The arm was straight. She did not complain this time. She lay staring at him, a frown between her eyes, her mouth slightly parted. There was no swelling. He said to the woman who stood by, her red-streaked eyes darting all over him, "You may pour cold water from the spout of your kettle over this arm each morning. It will restore tone to the injured parts and hasten the return of its use."

He removed a sliver from a toe belonging to a boy in the cluttered yard. And before he left, he was asked by the woman to examine an ailing cow. Doctor Tscharner refused. He mounted the black horse and rode away. The girl wandered to the yard and stood rubbing one bare foot over the top of the other and looking after him. He became a black blur in the dust. She looked at her arm. It was white and dead-looking, the flesh tender and vulnerable as a new mushroom. She held it to her nose and sniffed it cautiously.

It was ending the third summer that he had lived on Apion Mountain with his wife and child. He had added to his wealth and improved his holdings. The practice of his medicine spread throughout Larkin County and across the river into Weymouth. He rode to the patients. And they came to his surgery, some remaining to be nursed. There was no great friendliness.

He thought now of the corn he would harvest in September. As he rode from the ferry to Bloodworth's mill, kicking up a great dust, Doctor Tscharner remarked how dry the season had turned.

Aaron Bloodworth had dammed a mountain creek to operate his water wheel. The mill was well built and, though unpainted, gave off an air of wholesomeness. It was one place that seemed unblemished. Assuredly, the milldam, the overshot, the gates and sluiceway were all superimposed on the face of nature. But they were unassuming of their functions and waited for their power to come from the peculiar compromise of the water.

It was now a dry season and the millpond's surface was low. The wheel was not turning.

Bloodworth came out to greet him. He forked the horse some hay. He invited Doctor Tscharner to taste his corn whiskey, which he kept with him always in a greyish stone demijohn. Bloodworth was of a florid complexion with rather plain brown hair and hazel-colored eyes. The only remarkable aspect of his appearance was his set of good teeth, which he had managed to carry intact into manhood. Doctor Tscharner, accustomed to seeing carious teeth, blackened and broken, accompanied by the vilest breath, commented on the soundness of Aaron Bloodworth's teeth. The miller grinned and asked how he might preserve them, taking a noisy draw from the demijohn.

Tscharner surveyed him shrewdly. He arched his brows and, with an unusual spark in his eyes, he replied, "Tooth powders. Cinnamon, red bark, bicarbonate of soda mixed with pumice stone or charcoal and used each morning on a brush that has been dipped in warm water will keep your teeth like ivory and your breath as sweet as an infant's.

However"—he reached for the demijohn and poured himself a cup. Bloodworth listened intently, noting suspiciously the gleam in the doctor's eye. "However, my friend, to insure your own good teeth in your gums from now until the day of your demise, you should abstain from the drinking of hard liquors, which not only will ruin your teeth, but will also erode the coats of your stomach and cause you many sleepless hours of pain and repentance." Doctor Tscharner emptied the cup.

Bloodworth chortled and drew back the demijohn. He thumped it. "Thanky, Doctor," he answered. "I'll keep to my toothpick."

The floor was tracked in flour dust. Bloodworth kept a hired Negro, not a slave, sweeping the dust and another one flapping at the flies all day. Their names were Melachi and Bill. They stared at Doctor Tscharner.

"Ain't been no rain in a long spell. I caught all the water I could. Enough for two, maybe three hours' grinding. No moren that. We need rain." Bloodworth peered out the window at the sallow pond scummed with algae. Despite its stagnation, the pond still made a refreshing view. The oaks that grew around it arched into high domes. A meadow spread on the opposite side, blooming with daisies and red rudbeckia.

"If there ain't no rain soon, we going to be in a bad way." He turned back to Tscharner, grinning. "You know what them two niggers done?" He waved a hand at Melachi and Bill. They stopped sweeping and flapping and grinned back. "They run a big old blacksnake out from under the crib. Beat the hell out of 'im and hung 'im up on a mimosa tree." Bloodworth laughed. "That old blacksnake ain't harmed nobody. But them niggers is counting on 'im real hard."

Doctor Tscharner frowned. "I fail to see," he started. Bloodworth interrupted. "It's an old way. You kill a black-snake and hang it up in a tree and it'll bring rain." Bloodworth shook his head, still grinning. "I don't put no stock in it, but them niggers yonder believes!"

The doctor looked at the Negroes. They fell to sweeping and flapping flies. Bloodworth smacked at the flies crawling up and down his breeches. The backs of his hands were covered with reddish-brown hairs, and it seemed to Tscharner, though he could not be certain, that they sprouted from a hard layer of flour.

Bloodworth felt the black eyes travel over him and he resented it. He felt churlish, ill-bred. He threw up his hands and dismissed the calculating eyes with a "Goddamn it!" He glared back at Tscharner.

Doctor Tscharner smiled one of his rare pardoning smiles, recognizing a mettlesome man in this Aaron Bloodworth, a man with whom he could permit himself to fraternize. He got to the point of his visit.

"Last year, I bought flour from you and meal. It was clean, unspoiled. It lasted well."

Bloodworth nodded, soaking in the praise. "This year," continued the doctor, "I have corn of my own to be ground."

"Yeh, yeh." Bloodworth encouraged.

"I expect to harvest in late September, surely by the first frost. You had few coins to give me when I delivered your wife in May."

Bloodworth glanced up, curious at this.

"Grind my corn and consider it the balance." Doctor Tscharner cut short his proposition and bowed.

"I'll do it," replied the miller. He looked at the idle burr-stones. "If there's water left."

A little girl slipped in the door. She hurried to Bloodworth and whispered, eying the doctor. Bloodworth transferred the message. "Could you trouble yourself to stop off up at the house? Hannah Bloodworth needs a word with you. That baby, Fred Elbert's, been about to put her out of her wits with his colicking. She thinks you might can ease 'im."

Tscharner rode up the knoll that led to Bloodworth's house. It was planted in timothy. The spikes had grown to more than four feet, bending and springing back as though a single gigantic hand had pressed them down, then released them. The frame house was unpainted, but, like the mill below, it was clean-looking. The window glass sparkled and the chimneys had been freshly chinked.

The woman stood on the porch brushing with a bundle of broomstraw. She held the baby in the crook of her arm, almost burying his face against her large breast. She looked relieved to see Doctor Tscharner. Her face was bony and freckled, her hair stretched back in a tight knot. "Doctor." She began at once to complain while directing him inside and dumping the baby on the bed. The covers were drawn down so tightly that not a wrinkle or a crease could be seen anywhere. The child immediately began to wail and draw up his legs. "Doctor, there ain't been nothing but squalling from this child since the day he was born. The light ain't gone out at night in my house for near to four months. And my other baby, James is his name, he's been so jealous he runs a fever ever time he catches sight of me holding this-un."

Doctor Tscharner turned the baby over, pressing on his abdomen so that it was relieved all at once of its great flatulence. There were no febrile symptoms. "I suggest you immerse the child in a warm bath every time he suffers. Tie warm cloths around his belly. A little aniseed tea would give some relief. Steep it with flowers of benjamin." He prepared to go. "If you desire something stronger, send someone to my surgery and I shall dispense a bottle of paregoric elixir."

"Won't it get no better?" she asked, unsatisfied.

"He has what you might call growing colic. It won't get any better," Doctor Tscharner pronounced pitilessly.

"Then I'm sorry I ast," said Hannah Bloodworth. She scowled at the child on the bed. "What about my James?"

Tscharner looked at the sullen little boy who peered at them from around a cane-bottom chair. His lips were puffed out peevishly and his hair, which was quite red, drooped over his eyes.

"I have nothing for his illness."

He traveled toward Apion, his mind rippling over the person Aaron Bloodworth. He was disappointed in Bloodworth's wife. She was as common as the other wives he had observed in Larkin. But, he concluded ruefully, such characters would probably become the salt of the earth.

6

Ishmael's children annoyed Kaethe. The white eyeballs, faintly reddish in their corners, the dusty yarn twisted on the iron-colored pigtails, and the smell of small sweating bodies ignited a hideous emotion. She felt she must shriek, threaten them with a clenched fist. Instead, she said to them, "Good evening," her English faint and strange.

"Good evening, Miss," they replied. The pails of vegetables bumped against their legs, leaving ridges of dust on the black skin. The children had gathered late in the garden. The sun, low on the mountain, still sent out long fierce rays. She put up a hand. The bonnet was not enough. "Yes," she motioned them irritably, "yes. Go."

Their monkeyish fingers curled over the handles of the pails. A. D. scratched at his wool. The girls made simpering little curtsies and all three disappeared around the corner of the house. They left her with a great foolish feeling.

Kaethe sat in a swing made of planks and rope. She threw a blanket over the back to keep her dress from the splinters. It was the seventeenth day of August, 1828. Lieschen's third birthday. She thought he would have been there. But he was not. And now, late after the dinner had been cooked and eaten and all the plates washed, except for the one Pheny kept warming, he still had not returned.

She sat as she had sat for centuries, with Lieschen asleep on her lap. She sat staring at the darkening forest. She sat staring at the empty road. She sat pushing the clumsy swing with her feet and often fancied she could hear the crossing of the ferryboat, the dipping of wooden oars, or the swiftness of a skiff on the Council River. It was not hard. In her mind, the distance melted into nothing and the barest semblances of sound traveled unhampered.

She waited. The road grew dim under the black trees. The first stars appeared. Pheny came to take the child. The house settled. All through the early night, Kaethe sat staring at the blackness, the starlit, then the moonlit, waiting road. She roused suddenly, after hours had passed over her and she had been like a stone under water.

She felt a slight dizziness rise in her brain, a momentary clouding of all its bright running streams, and when she had blinked to regain herself, circles and circles of the brightest flame-colored light burst upon the black web of her consciousness. She felt nauseated and hurried to the edge of the porch and knelt down. Nothing would come to relieve her. Her stomach heaved, empty; her tongue felt heavy as a bar of lead. Perspiration sprinkled across her forehead.

She got up, grasping at the wooden post. Out in the black forest a swarm of fireflies bubbled, effervescent as white champagne. Before her numb eyes they danced and floated. Burst into bubbles, and then flew off like a swarm of panicked bees.

"Surely not," she whispered, wiping off the moisture with the hem of her skirt, unloosening the dark-blue basque. "It cannot be. I will not let it."

She fell forward into the flowers beside the stoop, screaming as she fell, and cursing the stems that broke under her, the bruised petals, the innocent green and feathery stamens.

Pheny came running. "Lawd! Lawd! Miss Katie!" She bent over Kaethe. She squatted down and looked at her. "What is the matter? You give me a fright. A terrible fright!"

Kaethe lay without answering. Then she turned her head so that she lay with her face toward Pheny's. "Get him, get him," she demanded.

At first the slave did not understand. Then the meaning slipped through her astonishment and she promised, "Yes'm, yes'm." She helped Kaethe to get up and go inside and to bed. Kaethe said no more. She lay on her bed calmly.

Pheny shut the door softly. She sat up until Doctor Tscharner came, toward midnight, the hoofs thudding in the white dust. He rode into the barn. Pheny ran out to him and told it, rubbing her arthritic finger joints nervously. He listened, fatigued, his dark eyes hazed. Then he turned without a comment and began taking off the harness. "Thank you, Pheny," he said. He took the lantern to the house. Its wide light washed across his boots.

Pheny went to Ishmael's cabin, and when she had told him of it, he shook his head and said, "Ain't nothing of ourn, woman. It his business and he'll see to it. Nothing of ourn."

They lay down and listened to the thumping of the insects against the sides of the cabin until they fell asleep, unafraid, breathing rhythmically.

The fits of hysteria came again, so many times she could not keep account of them. The repressions built under her broke loose without warning. At last she grew to recognize the hazy sickening preparations of her body and she would merely gasp and, as though acknowledging a familiar face, murmur, "Ah, yes, again."

The red cloud billowed inside her brain. Burning meteors attacked out of the dark innocent mass of her being. Pheny ran to her and held a singed feather under her nose. She drank a teaspoonful of assafoetida mixed in water. She alternately cried and laughed and beat her arms and legs. She felt that nails were being driven into her spine. She grabbed Pheny. "Whatever may happen, do not let him go away. Forbid him to leave." The frightened slave promised and promised.

The summer passed into autumn and the mountains were covered in red leaves. The leaves showered down and filled the valleys and covered the Kelly Star. The leaves flew up and scattered wildly as the horse dashed through them. The sickness that she had tried to quell proved too strong for her. She sought now to use it to advantage, to bind him to her. "You are not leaving, are you?" she would say to him after she had suffered a seizure. "Surely you will stay here to prevent the wanderings of my mind, to see that I shall not do harm to myself or Lieschen?" She picked at the bedclothes. Her voice was accusing.

"I am not insensitive to your plight, Kaethe," he replied. "I want to help you. Indeed, there is nothing I wish more than to stay here and attend your every need. But I cannot. Do not speak of it again. It does no good to continue hoping for the impossible."

He went away.

The corn was harvested and bound to stand in shocks for drying. Then it was gathered in the barn and shucked and that portion which was to be grist was shelled and put in sacks. Ishmael took it to the mill a little at a time and returned with the yellow meal.

Kaethe, stimulated by the change of season, determined she would take a new hand in the managing of her household. She rose earlier. But she found she did not like the dairying, the tying up of cheeses in bags, the churning. She fled from the butchering. The intestines that spilled from the hog and steamed in the frosty air mortified her. There was no place for her except in the kitchen. And she feared to go there, for she might be taken with a seizure and fall into the fire.

He knew that she needed cheerful company and amusements. He intended to see that she got them. He intended to give them. He left laudanum with proper instructions. He also advised lavender, a teaspoonful in a glass of wine when she felt the approach of the hysterics. He encouraged her appetite, especially in the eating of meat. She responded. She seemed to listen. He ordered a music box.

Kaethe began to write letters. The squeaking of the pen upon paper and the smell of the ink dispelled her languor. She wrote.

To Cécile Pons
Rue St. Etienne, Numéro 10
Pouvier
Loire et Cher

Darling Cécile,
But for my everlasting hope, I would not keep on. I say to myself, in the dead of the night, in the fairy-whisperings of the dawn, I sternly tell myself, "The letter was lost, scattered between here and Le Havre. Lost. She did not receive it."

Then with a swelling heart I add, "But perhaps this one will reach her." And to this I bolster my spirit with "For surely not all of hers have been doomed."

And thus I continue to write. I have doubts about the destinies of my letters. In this wilderness, the post service is not regular. I pay as far as New York. From there I cannot say what is the fate of my letters to you. Perhaps if I climbed to the pinnacles of these mountains and cried out my secrets to the green and empty forest, dearest sister, they might reach you as swiftly.

But, and this is my abiding strength, my Gibraltar rock, you have received my letters and thus you know my sentiment remains steadfast the same. A cold shudder runs over me as I press the pen to this paper. The truth is slow in arriving here to us in our seclusion. I hesitate. I do not wish to discover a new grief. I shudder. At least the veil is safe, this veil of unknowing. Silence, then, and distance, protect me. You are still there along with the others in Pouvier, all our good friends.

As for ourselves, we are the same brave three, Philip and Elisabeth and Jeannette. Philip's practice of medicine is our main means of livelihood. And it will make, we hope, with time, a comfortable fortune, if though small. Philip concerns himself with the estate and the cultivation of its gardens, the health and life of its woods, as seriously as he concerns himself with the afflictions, the lives and deaths of his patients.

This place wherein we live, if one were to go to the gaming table and cast down dice for it, would not retain us one further moment from you. Philip can never truly take for a fatherland this around us. But his lofty self-esteem, his pride in his skill, his need to prosper, consumes and destroys every bridge that I attempt to build across the sea.

Thus, I shall truly never see you again. Therefore, in view of my torment, it is wrong of you to ignore me, to deny me your letters, to refuse me what small sweet comfort your smallest words would bring to my impoverished heart.

But, come, I shall not take sides and quarrel. When one is as hopelessly banished, as am I, one grows to cherish all memories. The past will perhaps nevermore be.

A thousand sweet and tender things I send to you, none of which, I fear, will arrive.

Jeanne-Catherine P. Tscharner

She finished. The ink glistened on the paper, drying to a dull black. She folded the letter and wrapped it and wrote the address on the outside. It lay on the mantel for two weeks until Doctor Tscharner took it to Wharftown, four-teen miles upriver, across, and there posted it for New York.

He did not read the letters. And if he had, he would have destroyed them as unhealthy things.

It made her satisfied for a while to imagine them receiv-ing her letters in France. But the letters were not answered. She became angry, despondent, searching for a place to put the blame. Each person in Pouvier came before her mind and she searched suspiciously for the reasons why they would not answer her.

At last she stopped. She threw the last pages she had written into the fire. The paper swelled. It curled over and shattered.

Now she took each person and arranged him as she pleased. They did as she expected them to. They opened their mouths and spoke. She thought them all into and out of existence. She thought of Cécile. The game absorbed her in thousands of ways. In her mind, the child of perhaps seven took on the shape of a woman. Cécile became a woman as she herself had been in France at the time of her wedding.

She told Lieschen of Tante Cécile. She made a doll of rags and yellow yarn and drew a face on it with ink and called it *la poupée* Cécile. She gave it to the child. Lieschen looked at it. She took a finger out of her mouth and touched the face. The ink, absorbing the saliva from her finger, spread the doll's mouth into a crooked smile, then streaked across each side. Lieschen was delighted. She rubbed her wet hand over the doll's face. The eyes, the delicate nostrils, were obliterated by the black.

Then *la poupée* was snatched from her. "I hate you, you little snail! You little hare! I hate all of you! All!"

Kaethe rushed into her room and slammed the door. She held the ruined Cécile to her breast. Through the door, she heard Pheny coming to soothe Lieschen, who sat howling on the floor outside. She began to beat the doll against the door. "I will never go home. I will never go home. I will never go. Never. There is no point."

Then she stopped, horrified, catching sight of herself in the mirror that hung over the chest. Her red and smeary eyes soaked up and engorged themselves with the image: an unnatural mouth, trembling, bloodless, untidy strings of yellow hair, smudges of ink, and the tiny transparent tears that wiggled out of her eyes and slid down all over her face. A paralyzing revulsion spread over her. Her eyes widened, then closed. She fell backward across the bed, *la poupée* clenched in her fist.

7

The red leaves wilted and turned brown, rattling in the cold. Cones heaped up under the trees, brown and dry, vulnerable to sparks. The pine straw was thickened by more pine straw falling on top, adding weight to the dead dry mass. In the mornings, a thin shell of ice formed over the river. The ferryman's children cracked it into long pieces. They held it up, sharp and glittering, and sucked it. They ran across the frost with their red feet. They were afflicted with all the quinsies, putrid lungs, croups, and fevers of winter. Their mother interrupted Doctor Tscharner at his crossings and he went into the smelly house where ferocious fires roared on the hearths and the back corners of the rooms were damp and drafty. He ordered warm poultices, boneset teas, and forced lumps of brown sugar, tinctured with kerosene, down their phlegmatic throats.

The deer retreated deeper into the forest. The owl sought a hollow tree. At night the moon rose flat and bright against the black sky. Its whiteness illuminated the thickets where the deer huddled to get warm, their sharp hoofs crunching the crust of snow. The horned owl blinked and spread his wings. He cast himself upon the black air. He searched for mice, for ground squirrels, for anything that was small and ran upon the white ground. He flew without sound. The wind did not ruffle through his feathers. His horns were soft tufts over the merciless amber of his eyeballs. And when he had found his prey, he thrust his claws upon it and it was killed before it knew it had been caught.

Pheny heard the shrieking of the owl. She stopped poking at the fire and listened. The joints of her fingers began to hurt and she crawled back into bed, rubbing at them. "Ain't no good sign," she said to her husband, Ishmael. Her voice was low. "Bad owl. Hollering. You heard?" She nudged him in the rib.

Ishmael shifted his big feet and wound the covers tighter around his neck. "Yeh," he replied. "A killing owl."

Both lay quiet. Pheny gazed at the fire. The flames shot up suddenly, catching the soot. Lacey red sparks soared up the chimney, then the fire quietened. "The whole house under a bad sign," she said, "under a black dog."

Ishmael was asleep. His mouth dropped. He began to snore.

‡

On Apion Mountain, Kaethe dreamed she was cold. The air in the room was cold. Through the panes she saw the faint blue pallor of the snow. The forest was shrouded. Animals made small dark tracks, laboring fearfully in the snow, their dumb hearts quaking. Kaethe raised on an elbow. He was not there. He was never there. She called Pheny. The house rang with the cold. The crib where Lieschen slept was empty, the blue-blocked coverlet stretched smooth.

Kaethe called again, louder, then sank into the pillows. *So many pillows. White, soft, cold like snow.* She balled both hands into fists and pounded her eyeballs. Her body began to swell. Her ribs arched as the lungs beneath them inflated with terrific pressures. Her body became a bellows, sucking up the air, grabbing fistfuls of snow and dust and cold black air. She ballooned to the top of the room. Then something restrained her.

A dark arm held her down. He had leeches, pale, transparent leeches, to suck at her. He burned out a cup to draw the blood. It was a wine cup. She thought gaily, "How odd. It is a wine cup. It is made of glass and I can see the blood beneath it." She felt elated.

He displayed the lancet with its swift steel edge. He knew the art of bloodletting, of opening veins and closing them back up. It was an art. She was gay. Her blood sang under his thumb. Easily she poured out sixty ounces, a hundred, through the vein he had chosen. Then he began to bind her.

She did not wish to be through so soon. She pounded her fists harder. The air was gone. The bed was as frail as a dead leaf. The flakes fell again. They piled up on the windows and filled the dark tracks in the field.

✝

Doctor Tscharner had gone to ease whatever ailed them. Red throat, fevers, the pang of childbed. Kaethe dreamed again. She held a yellow tea rose from his garden. She thought it strange to find roses in his garden, an unproductive odorous rose. The yellow petals unfurled in long yellow flames. They merged into one flame, clear and bright as a star. It burned steadily. Cécile began to sing.

> He shivers on the musty straw,
> Jesus, that sweet and heav'nly child.
> The ox, the ass upon him blow,
> To keep him warm with breathings mild.

The song disintegrated into white flakes and swirled like snow. Cécile smiled. The Epiphany candle she carried burned itself away. The yellow wax overflowed and dripped on her fingers. She threw it down, crying. Kaethe went to her, full of words, but the child vanished. The yellow candle was absorbed by the snow.

Far out in the darkness, a wild creature shrieked. She shuddered and hugged herself. The dream obliterated itself.

She awoke. She had drawn the bedclothes around her face. He was not back. The air in the room was colder and blacker. It was so cold, Kaethe felt it might have a surface, a skin, which she could touch and find slick as china.

She got out of bed and walked across the room to look at Lieschen. The floor was icy. She bent over. Lieschen was warm, curled in a fetal ball, intense with sleep. The warmth of her rose up and steamed off Kaethe's coldness. She smelled of urine, warm and yellow, a nesting odor.

71

Kaethe moved back. She moved from this room and down the middle of the house, her eyes fixed straight in front of her. She unlatched the door.

"Philip, Philip." The snowy mountains threw back her shrill cry. "A bone to a dog, a bone to a dog," she whispered, "throw me a bone." Her face burned in the bitterness and her lips came apart. Her teeth danced on her tongue like clogs of ice.

Would he never return? "Philip!" The blade was sinking up to its helve. She wanted him there. "Why cannot I be eased?" she shouted.

"Diseased, diseased," the cry threw back, hollow and cold.

She leaped into the snow. "Philip," she struggled, "you liar!" Her ankles would not sustain her. She plunged down the slope and fell hard. She lay studying what had happened, calculating it in rainbow-colored flashes. Then she whirled furiously on her cold belly and beat at the snow. The balloon lifted her like the moon that hung round and stupid behind dark pines.

Pheny's screaming cracked open the thin morning and brought the others running. Kaethe lay drowned in snow. They carried her into the house. She was wet to the bone. The strands of her hair were frozen. And when Pheny peeled away the nightdress, pieces of red skin peeled away with it.

Ishmael shouted to his boy, "Saddle up and fetch him. You be quick!"

The boy, riding an old plow mule, met Doctor Tscharner four miles down the road. A. D. was so frightened that his voice would not open. He slid down and stood blubbering and pointing back until he finally got out two intelligible sounds, "Miss Katie!" Doctor Tscharner reached down and swung A. D. up on the horse before him. The old muie, neglected, stood for a moment, then obediently followed in a slow jog.

Snow scattered under the horse. Over Apion, the diminishing moon blinked owlishly in the new glare of the sun. Wind stung Doctor Tscharner's face. A. D. sobbed against his chest.

He could not revive her. She was deader than anything he had ever touched with his hands. He lifted her, unbelieving that this muddy snow smell belonged to her. The head wobbled, too heavy now for her neck. The hair, drawing color from the dying tissue, gleamed. All of her gleamed. The cold slick skin gave off a definite light.

Or so it seemed to Doctor Tscharner, who sat with his dead mate in his arms in a room reflecting the snow. He sat on the muddy disturbed bed and watched through the small window with its streaked glass. The scene beyond was not changed. Not one dimension of it altered.

At noon, he allowed Pheny to come into the room again.

8

Two days she remained on the bed. She was washed. She was dressed. He cut up a camphor gum and dissolved it in brandy. Pheny wrung out cloths dipped in the stuff and wiped the dead one's face. Camphor and brandy would keep her white until they got her buried. Pheny tied his largest handkerchief around the head, up from under the chin, to hold its lips shut.

It snowed again and covered the ground with new whiteness. Doctor Tscharner sat in the surgery and watched it fall. And when it had stopped, the sky became as smooth as slate. He decided that loneliness was not a healthy thing for him while she lay in the house. The slaves he could not join. His patients knew nothing of his grief. Even had they known of it, they would have been no more to him than centipedes that crawl across the toes of the Sphinx. There were many things in Aaron Bloodworth of which Doctor Tscharner could not approve. But he sought him out.

The millpond was grey under ice. The black trees were coated with ice. And the overshot wheel hung in long icicles. The mill was empty. He went up the slope to the house. Bloodworth let him in and invited him to the fire. The children shelled popcorn. They held it over the fire in a wire basket with a long handle and squealed when the kernels exploded or caught on fire. The woman Hannah sat chuckling, her face red from the warmth. Her baby sat with the hem of his dress under a bedpost to prevent him crawling into the fire. He played contentedly with a wooden spoon.

Bloodworth set out the demijohn. Doctor Tscharner took a long pulsating draft. He sat for a moment, absorbing this room, the sounds of the exploding grain, and he marveled at its solar system that traveled different orbits from his own. Then he told Bloodworth of the death.

"I'll come," said Aaron Bloodworth. He held up a hand. "I know you ain't ast me. But I'll come anyhow. Ain't no cause bear it alone now."

He returned with Doctor Tscharner and they sat in the surgery with the demijohn on the table between them. Bloodworth was curious to go in and see her, but he became more curious about the things the doctor began to tell him, things of the sea, of his crossing, things of the European world. Bloodworth forgot all about the dead until

Tscharner said resignedly, after a long time, "She must be buried."

"You got to fetch old man Lentz."

"He is not the one to bury her." Doctor Tscharner scowled. Then he relaxed, agreeing, "Yes, you are right."

A. D. was sent to Rocky Run. Lentz set his face against the wind and beat his horse down the snow-blurred ditches. Brown dry brambles rattled as he passed.

He dismounted at the foot of the slope and led the horse. The frozen, convoluted Kelly Star Road was strewn below. Doctor Tscharner's grey house hovered like a large bird. The chimneys were smoking. A slave came to take his horse. The door opened. Doctor Tscharner stood looking down at the preacher with cold black eyes in which the man could see no sign of sorrow. Lentz felt he must speak. He swept off his hat and said, falteringly, "God bless you, my neighbor, in this loss of your beloved." He stopped. Doctor Tscharner stood looking. Lentz said again, this time not looking, "God bless you." When he had finished, he was taken into the house. He was surprised to see Aaron Bloodworth.

"Where is the deceased one?" he asked, stealing a glance around.

"In her coffin," replied Bloodworth, inwardly rejoicing in the preacher's discomfiture.

"But —" Lentz was stupefied—"but there ain't been no prayers said over the body, no witnessing."

Doctor Tscharner gazed at the coffin, which was nailed shut, supported on a plank between two chairs. "It is not proper that my dead be looked upon." He fixed the short soft preacher with his black stare. "Begin."

Lentz hastily placed his hands upon the lid of the coffin, closed his eyes, and began reciting the Lord's Prayer, which was the first thing that occurred to him, not at all what he would have chosen. Near the end, he cracked his eyes to look at Doctor Tscharner and was mortified to find the doctor staring hard at him, his head unbowed. "Amen," said Lentz. "Amen," repeated Bloodworth.

Ishmael and Clegg and A. D. and Aaron Bloodworth lifted the coffin from the plank. At the door, Doctor Tscharner stepped forward. He led them out of the house, through the farmyard and across a clear running stream, banked in snow, to the cemetery in the woods. The ground had been opened with axes. Ishmael fastened ropes around the coffin and they lowered it into the red hole. Lentz, like an afterthought, hurried forward. He scooped up a handful of the cold earth and dropped it on the disappearing coffin, chanting his specialized words. He pulled a handkerchief out of his pocket to wipe away the mud from his fingers.

It began to snow. The flakes melted as they touched the moist earth. Doctor Tscharner motioned them all away. They left him. At the house, Lentz prepared to go. But before he mounted he glared at Aaron Bloodworth and said, "Bloodworth, I smell likker on your breath."

Bloodworth stretched out his arms, cracking the knuckles of his fingers. He grinned. "Yeh," he said, "you do."

They left the place of Philip Tscharner. The snow was bad.

It was not many days after this that the music box he had ordered for her arrived. It had a crank on the side and he wound it up once for Lieschen to hear.

77

On his next ride to Wharftown, he left instructions with a stonecutter for an obelisk. It was hauled in on the back of a wagon in March, as the earth was thawing and a slush ran, choking the road. The four sides tapered into a white pyramid. On one of the sides was chiseled in thick sensible unadorned letters:

JEANNE-CATHERINE PONS

Beloved of Philip Tscharner of Jutta, Germany

BORN APRIL 2, 1806   DIED JANUARY 11, 1829

NIGHTSHADE

9

"Jake Pons," affirmed Aaron Bloodworth, "was so god-damned stingy he'd dry up a flea for his hide and tallow and walk across hell on a hair for his cracklings."

"Don't say such things," said his wife. They sat on the porch of the mill, where greenish sun speckled the air. Bloodworth's face was redder than usual because he was eloquently drunk. The surface of the pond was dusted with a yellow pollen from the oaks. The overshot turned with a mighty rush of water.

"Them niggers has got my gate up too high," he thundered in Hannah's ear. He tramped inside. "Melachi! Lower that gate a damned fraction." Bloodworth inspected the burrstones. The hard greyish-white discs were too close. The upper one struck occasional sparks as it grated against its mate. "Melachi!"

The Negro ran in, his clothes wet from the spray of the overshot. "Yawser," he said. Bloodworth painted dramatically. "Look at them rocks. You trying to burn 'em up?"

"Nawser." Melachi shook his head and looked frightened as the quick sparks grated off the siliceous grooves.

"Then I strongly suggest that you spread 'em a bit. I ain't paying you to burn up my rocks. And folks ain't paying me to grind up ashes."

He returned to Hannah on the porch. "I told you how he done 'em, ain't I? Not long after Shanner's woman died, old Jake up and died hisself, and when the will-reading was held, he'd left both Shanner and the youngun no moren fifty cents apiece! How's that for you?" Bloodworth swelled.

"I don't believe it." Hannah wrinkled her nose at him. The baby slept in her lap and she fanned the flies from his face. "Besides, Shanner ain't grooming no grudges. Now not, leastways. Not after she's gone."

Bloodworth looked at her irritably. Her practicality appalled him. And, as if divining exactly how to chafe his discontent, she added in a cheerful, practical, reassuring, and damnable way, "What I'm wondering is why don't he take that child and go back. Seems like a man would want to settle with his blood family, with his friends." She chuckled and pulled the baby's dress smooth, rubbing away the wrinkles, inspecting the spots. "You know he's got the money to do it."

"Ain't nobody knows nothing." Aaron Bloodworth

turned in his chair and stared over the meadow. He listened to the spilling of the water through the wheel. The wooden dam that held back the pond had turned dark and slick and was furred with thick healthy mosses. There was at least a nine-foot drop from the top. It soothed him to see his dam holding back the water. He did not talk any more to his wife, but went inside and examined the brown meal. It passed, vibrating, along a wooden trough from the burrstones and was bolted through a piece of screen wire. It collected into a barrel, fine flour, brown and sweet-tasting, ground from the whole kernel. The bran and chaff were saved for fodders. He helped the Negroes sew it into sacks. By the time they finished, shadows had fallen over the water and the meadow was dark. Bloodworth set the mill in order and went home.

His wife had stewed a chicken and made pastries to go in it. She ladled his plate full of meat and golden juice. The pastries floated. After his supper, Aaron Bloodworth felt jovial. He ruminated on Doctor Tscharner and swigged from the demijohn. The tall dark man had stopped many times to rest at the mill, to talk with him. They talked of strange things, things that Bloodworth had never thought of before but which, once he had turned them in his mind, tantalized him and made him exasperated with his nearsightedness. He had been out of Larkin County only once, when he went on a journey with his father to the capital, Raleigh. It had taken two days and nights to go and two more days and nights to return. They had cooked their supper in a three-legged pot and slept under the wagon.

Hannah clattered the plates, blurring his reflections.

"I know one thing," he told her, his healthy teeth flashing. "If the world is as big between here and where Shanner come from as it is between here and Raleigh, it's a goddamned jolly whopper!"

She sniffed. She was not amused. Her back hurt and the greasy plates depressed her. "You think what he says is so. Then why does he stay stuck here all the time?" She threw the last plates in the dishwater. It sloshed and spattered on her feet. " 'Cepting you," she said, "he ain't got no friends to speak of."

Bloodworth stopped grinning. "Something I learned, woman, and that is a man don't need a whole gob of friends. Friends!" he scoffed. "You think I got friends?"

"Well, yes. Course," she began weakly, floundering to recapture her position. "There's Darley that's your friend. And Hosea Squires. And Trasker at Wharftown."

"Barsh!" he scattered her arrangement. "They ain't friends. There ain't a one amongst them that you calls friends but what wouldn't do me in ifen they got the chanct. And I ain't saying I wouldn't do them the same. Ifen *I* got the chanct. Barsh!"

Hannah noticed for the first time the children, who began to line each side of the table, turning their round freckled faces from one parent to the other, absorbing their words. Charlotte, Ramona, Mary June, James, with his thatch of red hair: their fingers tapped on the wet table, they breathed through their mouths. It threw her into a terrible temper. "Oh, Aaron!" she erupted, "how can you be so *con*trary?"

10

It was still cold. The first day of May hung grey and wet over the mountain, dripping from pines. Lieschen ran scrambling on her short legs along the peeled logs that led from the house out to the kitchen. At the end of the logs a round smooth river stone was set into the ground. It stood as high as the logs but a step lower than the sill of the kitchen. The door was shut and she could not reach the latch. She beat on the door with her fists, and when no one opened it, she began to cry.

The cold spring air clouded on the eaves of the roof, making drops of water collect and run down the small panes of the window. Pheny peered out the window but she could not see Lieschen, who stood so small on the stone. Lieschen beat upon the door again and howled bitterly, Pheny opened the door and grumbled to herself. When she saw that it was the child, she scooped her up in her skinny arms and said, "Lawd, it 'uz Lizzie making all that racket."

She slammed the door behind them and set the child down before the crackling fire. "Yo hand's as cold as a little pig's foot!"

Lieschen pulled her hands away from Pheny and ran over to look on the table. "I want to see the rock," she demanded.

"Hah?" asked the Negro.

"Ish say you cooking a rock. I want to see you cooking a rock." She scowled at Pheny, who scowled back at her, blinking her eyes like a bird, a black hand cupped around her ear. "Hah?"

"A rock! A rock!" howled Lieschen. "Ish say it! Ish say a rock!"

Pheny got a long pan off the table and showed it to the child. "Ain't no rock, honey. *Fish!* Fish is what Ish catched in the rock shallers. Rockfish, honey. Basses. Rock basses. Look here. See 'em in there all skint and ready for the skillet?"

Lieschen looked in the pan, then screwed up her face and began a fresh weeping. Pheny put the fish back on the table and, taking Lieschen on her lap, sank into her rocker in the corner of the kitchen. The child was streaked with tears and her nose bubbled mucus. She had wet herself and smelled of urine. Pheny took a rag from her apron and began to clean Lieschen's face. "When he going to take him a woman? When, in the Lawd's time, he going take him a new woman?"

Doctor Tscharner did not think of women. The facts of his life arranged themselves and he obeyed. He moved his things into the surgery after his wife's burial and slept there. Pheny and Rutha kept Lieschen amused and fed. They put food before him when he came and he ate it. Ishmael and his son and Clegg prepared the land and planted the seeds according to their seasons as he had ordered. He wrote a letter to the family of Pons in Pouvier informing them of the death of their daughter. He did not ask for replies.

He wrote another to his family in Jutta. It was the first letter he had written to them since coming to America and he saw that it would also be the last. He was brief and to the point.

To the Family of my father:

We were foolish to have pinned hopes onto vapor. The rich uncle of Jeanne-Catherine P. proved false in his promises. I have luckily provided us with food and the comfort of a small estate. In the beginning it was about one hundred and forty morgen, but now I have increased it to almost twice. And it is legally mine.

Should one of you consider coming here to try your luck, make certain that you have a practical trade. This land holds no uses for musicians, dancing masters, drawing teachers, and the like. If you are married, do not consider coming at all. Your woman would not fare well. There are no Germans here. I am the local scarecrow.

However, if one of you must come to see for yourself, then I will stand steadfast by you as a brother.

My wife, Jeanne-Catherine P. of Pouvier, died of extreme exposure to the cold on the eleventh of January, 1829. I have buried her here on my estate. My daughter, Elisabeth Tscharner, and I are in health and send you our greetings.

P. Tscharner
May 1829

His days were not spent in idleness. He worked in the sticky warm air of the plant shed, encouraging the swelling and struggling of new buds to gain the light. And when he was tired of the plant shed, he sought the surgery and set himself grinding powders, distilling spirituous medicines over the Bunsen. He sat at the daybook and balanced debits against credits. He sickened of the enclosure and went out to labor with his slaves. He took off his black cape and hung it from a tree limb. He stood in the dirt and swung a hoe in the rows. He crumbled the dirt around the plants. The slaves no longer worried at his approach in their territory. He went with A. D. to gather pine knots for the kitchen fires. He labored hard in the light of day, and at night he slept well. And he did not mind being roused by Ishmael's rough hands in the dead of sleep. "Doctor Shanner, wake! Master Marsh here."

He did not mind rousing and dressing, gathering the saddlebags, riding down the sides of Apion Mountain. The dark thick branches drooped over him. Streams of water flashed in the black earth. He rode silently, as if asleep, to attend Marsh's wife, who suffered with consumption, to attend the children of Trasker in Wharftown, who choked with asthma, to deliver the daughters of Ritchie Coe from their Magdalene fruits.

Doctor Tscharner rode through Apion forest. His eyes squinted. He trusted the big dark animal beneath him. At the foot of the mountain, the horse turned to follow cumbersome paths, his hoofs knocking aside the white pebbles. The gleaming Council River wound like a snake through the trees. He came awake. Everywhere he could see the moon. It lined every branch of every tree and sprang at him from the brush. The air was not cold. It teemed with light. He smelled cedar. He smelled crushed green needles. He smelled the flashing water. The horse began to gallop over the Kelly Star.

In the shallow-ceiled little houses, miserably blackened, he waited through the progressions of labor with the Magdalene daughters. They shrieked at him and cursed him and confessed to him. He gave them no more attention than they deserved, seeing to it that the bearing-down was not obstructed, that the separation of the navel string was not done too soon, and that the bleeding was stopped. He took no notice of the infants, handing them to the midwives who hovered behind him like winged roaches batting at a flickering lamp.

In the clean, swept, polished house of Marsh, he examined the dying woman, who lay with her lungs full of blood. "Is Ma going to die?" asked a boy at his elbow, blinking moon-shaped blue eyes.

"Yes," replied Doctor Tscharner, "she is dying this moment."

He gave laudanum to the choking children of Trasker and ordered a poultice of benjamin leaves. By then it was morning and cold. It would warm up by noon, but now it was a clear, granite-colored cold, echoing with bird calls.

He got on his horse and rode by the river. The yellowish water dashed against the bracken. River birches with glistening trunks bent over the river. Spiderwort had sprouted in the thickets. When he got home to Apion, he went to the surgery and fell asleep again without removing his clothes. He did not deplore his lack of friends. He did not trouble himself with his kinsmen in Europe. He did not meditate upon women. Such things did not signify in the mind of Doctor Tscharner.

He concentrated upon real signs. His wheat survived the cold winter. His slaves flailed it. And he took it to the miller to be ground and bolted into flour. His seedlings were taking firm root. Doctor Tscharner did not intend to vegetate monotonously.

But some several years passed in this way, undisturbed, with the adhesion of lichens.

11

The seasons wound themselves in a fine tensile spool. Summer, dead leaves, snow, the first shad. The thread was stretched thin and bright as gold. The passing of time was cold or hot, it was flayed off as easily as the hide of pigs in hot water. It was soporific, comforting.

Cassandra Keith fitted into the weave of things. At seventeen, she did not have many dreams. She did not dream of Doctor Tscharner. There were many in Larkin County who did. They lay and dreamed of black Tscharner riding in the wind, tossing them through the dark, dividing them in two, hacking and clefting, grinding their roots like powder in his mortar. Cassandra Keith was not honored with dreams like these. She was a light sleeper, ready to wake at any moment, lying always on her side, both knees drawn up to her breast.

She was not pretty at seventeen and she had a scar on her face, below the left eye, where Jonah had hit years ago with a hoe. "Lucky it didn't take her eyeball out," scolded her ma, mopping at the blood flooding the girl's cheek, brightly staining her dull hair. "How come you do such a thing, Jonah?"

Jonah stood with the hoe across his shoulder, like a rifle. "She ast for it! She ast for it! Always in my way!"

This wound should have been sutured with a needle and well-waxed thread. But the mother dashed water over it, stunning the blood, and plastered on a goo of thorn apples until it had formed an ugly hard scab. And when the scab fell away, Cassandra wore a small white crescent that would not tan in the sun.

She did not care about the scar, for she did not go about peering into mirrors at herself. To have come upon her reflection in a mirror would have struck her as silly and unnatural and she would have been scornful. She took her physical existence for granted. Shoved about by her brothers, struck in the face, scratched, she did not puzzle her appearance on the surface of the planet any more than she would have puzzled the appearance of a fly or mushroom.

As a child, she never clung to her mother's skirt. That mother was fat and red in the face and her skirt was filthy with grease or blood. And the smell of her armpits was unpleasant. Her father showed her no special favor. He lived with the river and he knew it better than he knew himself, its rise and fall, its currents, its eddies. The cables creaked overhead, pulling the ferry at an angle so that it took full advantage of the river's flow downstream. Keith talked and joked with his passengers. The river was narrow at this crossing. He claimed he could spit across to the Weymouth side. He paid no attention to the land.

Keith's sons were unrooted. They put seeds in the land as their mother bullied them. They came to the table and put their feet under it and ate. And when their fat, red, bullying mother died, they came to the table as always and partook of the funeral repast. And in the months that followed, they drifted away and were dispersed to the directions of the wind. There were left behind only three. There was left Jonah, who spent his days digging for gold along the banks of the river and who swore that he would light out and leave when he found it. There was left the girl Cassandra. And there was left one small boy, of about seven or eight, called Boone. These three constituted the family of the ferryman Keith.

Cassandra sat in the house on the riverbank and looked at its grey splintered walls. The ceilings were high and dark and there were many rooms. A bucket of water stood on a table near the door. The dipper was made from a gourd and it hung from a nail in the wall. She kept a cloth spread over the bucket, but flies continued to congregate around the rim and crawl over the gourd. They settled on Cassie. She enjoyed the sensation of their feathery legs and allowed them to crawl halfway up her arm before she slapped at them, crushing their bodies. She wiped the sticky mess from her fingers.

Days and nights followed each upon the other and took no notice of this Cassandra Keith. And she, in turn, calculated only the flowing of her menstrual blood. She planted a soup garden on Good Friday, the last of April, as her ma had always insisted upon, in the back of the house. She made Jonah plow it. "Where you want it?" he bellowed, standing behind the plow, jerking at the mule. "Where?" His big red hands, exactly like her bullying ma's, gripped the plow handles. She glared back at him from the door. "There," she said, pointing at the ground below her feet, below the door stoop, "right there!"

And he plowed it there, slicing through the dirt, the mule's rump bumping up against the side of the house. He plowed there as she had told him. The rows came right up to the door, right under her foot.

"Damn you," she hissed under her breath as he passed.

She put on her bonnet made from sacks, took a bag of seed and a hoe, and, instructing Boone to follow, trudged through the new-turned dirt. She scooped back the dirt with her hoe and Boone dropped in the seed and she pushed back the dirt, tamping it with the flat of the hoe.

May was a wet cold month. It had been wet and cold in May for many years. But it had accomplished itself and the garden was not harmed. In June it grew hotter and flies and stinging insects swarmed from the river. It grew so hot, she thought she could not breathe for choking on dust and mosquitoes. Beans appeared in her garden, the corn tasseled, she gathered okra and squash, onions multiplied and multiplied into hundreds of bulbs underground.

In the evenings before dark, while the sun was still spreading through the sky, Cassandra left the grey house and went to the river. She went through the woods, following a deer trail upstream. Wild grape grew all around her, tangling from the trees, the new green tendrils curled as tight as watch springs. Bugbane thrust its white spikes through the brown straw. The woods were rich, the earth spongy to her naked feet, and when she had gone far enough to be safe, she climbed down to the river and waded.

She leaned forward and pushed herself under. The water felt sickeningly warm and she was disappointed. When she broke the surface a body's length away from the point of her immersion, the dress stuck to her skin and her hair was plastered dark down. She stripped off the dress and wrung the water from it. She waded back to the bank and spread the dress over a bush. She turned on her back and floated, looking at the sky. It was a clear ashy blue, as though everything had been burned away and only this blueness left. For as far as she could see in either direction, there were no clouds to disturb it. She floated naked in the water and the sky floated over her, naked and blue. She did not want to leave where she was.

A flock of birds flew off from the trees making noisy cries, rupturing the serenity.

Cassandra came out of the water, squeezing her hair as she walked. A thread of water streamed between her breasts. Her legs glistened. Minnows darted in the shallows and great swarms of mosquitoes rose out of a clump of horsemint. She put on the dress, and by the time she returned to the house, it was drying, wrinkled around the hem, and her hair felt scratchy. The mosquitoes bit her and she raked at the skin until it bled.

Sometimes she took Boone with her to the river. She was not ashamed to be naked before him. But she did not want him to touch her with his little boy's hands. He dived under the water and gathered himself into a ball. Then he unloosened and hung there limply, his arms drifting with the current.

"Boonie." Cassandra bent above him. He could hear her voice coming strained through the water. Her small breasts swung over her ribs. Beads of water clung to the roseate nipples and through the skin a blue vein pulsated dimly. He sprang up and pinched her.

"Boonie!" The slap she gave him cracked out louder than thunder and her fingers left a row of red welts. She stalked out of the river leaving him half-drowned and stupidly grinning, wallowing in the silt.

The mosquitoes became more intense. They hung in clouds over the river. They came in through the windows and stung her. She could not refrain from clawing at the bites until they bled and formed sores. Her legs and ankles were dotted with these sores. She picked at them in her sleep. She picked and scratched and the blood was saturated with the dirt from her fingernails and the stinging acid of the mosquitoes.

She became ill in the night and felt worse in the morning. She drank deep draughts from the water bucket, but could not be assuaged. By evening of the next day, Cassandra could not lift her head from the bed. A heavy and uncommon rain poured down all night, and when it had stopped, a great mist exuded from the river and through the low woods. It smelled of the river and of rotting leaves.

Cassandra was afire. Her father told Jonah to take her to Doctor Tscharner and leave her. If the fever was catching, he wanted her out of the house. "She's got the creeping miasma," he said, "and it's worse than the sores of Job. Get 'er from here!"

She was cold, yet she complained of great internal heat. They could not remove the blankets she had wrapped about herself. Jonah carried her downstairs draped over his shoulder like a sack of meal and laid her in the wagon. He took her to Doctor Tscharner and he commanded, "You get her cured."

And he left without a back look to see if they took her in out of the weather.

12

Clegg tipped the candle over a bucket and allowed some hot wax to collect in the bottom. Then he settled the candle firmly in the wax and waited while it hardened.

"You got that candle fixed?" asked Ishmael.

"Yeh, but who going go down that well? Not me." Clegg handed the bucket over to Ishmael, who began to lower it carefully. It was a big candle and the flame flickered in the depths, reflecting off the sides of the bucket and the wet rocks. "It burning," he solemnly reported.

"Let it down some mo," said A. D., peering over the

curb. "That a deep well, Pappy. It go down into the very bowels of the earth."

Ishmael unwound the rope slowly. The windlass whined. The three Negroes peered into the dark wellhole. Drops of sweat popped out on their heads. "It sho sultry," remarked Clegg. He stood back from the well and wiped his face.

"Yeh," replied A. D. "That how come them wigglers down there."

There was a soft plop as the bottom of the bucket touched water.

"It still burning?" asked Clegg, peering over again.

"Yeh." Ishmael began to turn the windlass in reverse. "I going bring 'er back up again." He turned and they watched as the bucket rose up the dark hole silently bearing the burning candle. He brought it to the top and pulled it over and set it down. "Go tell Doctor Shanner ain't no foul air down his well. The candle still burning and I going keep it burning till he come see for hisself."

A. D. hurried across and knocked at the door of the surgery. Doctor Tscharner opened it no more than a crack. He held a wet cloth over his mouth. A. D. tried to catch a glimpse of the white girl who lay inside and who was the cause of them having to clean the well. Doctor Tscharner followed the boy, still holding the cloth in front of his mouth when he spoke. Ishmael pointed to the candle in the bucket. "See. It burning. It burned all the way down and all the way back up."

"Put it down again," directed the doctor. "The test must be made twice to be proven true. Maybe even a third time."

Ishmael began to lower the bucket again. "I knowd you

going say that," he murmured sulkily. It disappeared, the candle flickering. Doctor Tscharner watched it descend. Ishmael raised it, still burning, then repeated the task. He waited for the doctor's decision.

"All right," he said, speaking through the wet cloth. A sharp aromatic odor came from it. "It must be pure. It should be safe enough for a man." He turned to go back to the surgery. "You may proceed." He went away, the smell of the sickness going with him. He went into the surgery and shut the door severely.

Ishmael looked at Clegg and A. D. "Awright. Who going go down?"

"Not me, brother," affirmed Clegg. "I can't stand no such as that. I can't stand going down no dark holes. I going hold the meer. Somebody got to hold the meer."

"I reckon I going go," said A. D. in a martyr's tone. "You too stout, Pappy." He gazed at Ishmael. "Ise slight of build. I going go. But I ain't unless *you* holds the rope, Pappy."

Ishmael nodded. "We done drawed all the water we can. You got to bail out the rest. You understands?"

A. D. sighed and went to the kitchen, where Rutha wound wadding around his shoulders and chest. They had assembled an apparatus of ropes and pulleys with which to lower him down and then hoist him up again. Ishmael buckled the straps to him. Clegg angled the mirror to catch the rays of the sun and reflect them down the well so that A. D. might have light to see.

They lowered him down, a bucket clutched in his arms. When he touched bottom, he sank up to his ankles in cold mud. "Jee-zus!"

"What wrong?" called Ishmael.

"Nothing." A. D.'s answer spiraled up, reverberating faintly off the glistening rocks in the wall of the well. "That meer sho is bright. Lemme have that hawghead."

Ishmael sent down the hogshead. It blacked out A. D.'s light as it descended and he feared he would be utterly crushed like an ant. It settled clumsily into the mud and he filled it with the water and slime and sent it back. The mirrored sun bounced off the shiny infested water. He felt mosquitoes sting his legs and arms and face. The smells of the water and the mud and the darkness were like no other smells he had known. He was in a perilous new region, a dimension of blackness and softness, cold and stinging. "How long I going be down here, Pappy?" he called as the hogshead banged down again.

"Till you got all that wiggler slop bailed," replied Ishmael. His big head was as insignificant as a pimple on the rim of the wellhole. A. D. felt his own insignificance acutely, as a stab of pain, and in order to displace it, began bailing rapidly.

The water seeped in constantly. It percolated through the mud, sucking and gurgling at his feet. By the end of the morning, he had sent up ten barrels of muddy water, gallons and gallons of slime bubbling with larvae. Then he was drawn up and he lay stunned on the grass, blinking at the black mud drying to grey, his body throbbing from the ropes.

Pheny and Rutha poured great quantities of boiling water down the well until they had satisfied Doctor Tscharner that the mosquitoes were destroyed.

He knew nothing of yellow fever, of malaria. He only knew the fever the girl suffered was malignant and dangerous and that in some subtle way it had to do with her habits of bathing in the river and with the acrid sores on her legs. He had found larvae in his well water and, while he had no proof the insects would do him harm, had ordered their destruction. Now he allowed the well to fill again, convinced the water would be clean. He had cured the water. He had yet to cure the malignant girl.

She lay on a straw pallet while he forced the fever to expire. She suffered paroxysms of chills followed by fever and extreme sweating. She was afflicted with retching, vomiting up phlegm and bile. After this, she would fall into a sleep.

He gave strong emetics and purged her bowels of the malignancy that had settled there. She then passed into the second stage of the fever and became very hot, her pulse strong and tense. She called for water and demanded to be fanned. She pulled at her clothing and threw off the blankets she had clung to in her chill.

Pheny came to help him bleed the girl. He tied a ligature tightly above the elbow. When the vein was conspicuous, he placed his left thumb an inch below the place where he wished to puncture her. Holding the lancet firmly, he made an incision obliquely into the vein and kept his hand steady, fearless, never raising the handle.

When he had drawn off as many ounces as he thought safe, he instructed Pheny to untie the ligature. He put his thumb this time on the incision and pressed it shut. He applied a linen compress over the wound and upon this he placed another compress and yet another, until he had filled the hollow space in the bend of her arm. His long fingers drew a strip around the elbow in a figure eight, passing through the pattern many times. He finished by tying a knot over it all.

The candle flickered at night and threw long shadows over the walls. The candle melted and remelted, overflowed itself and ran down to collect and cool in the stick. Doctor Tscharner sprinkled her with cold water and vinegar. Pheny brought cracked ice and placed it between her lips and under her arms. He succeeded in warding off the final and most morbid stage of her fever, that of the black vomit.

For a while, Doctor Tscharner was uncertain of his cure. The girl said nothing. The eruptions faded from her skin. The fever expired as he had wished and her stupor began to diminish. Her hair came out in long dull brown tufts. Pheny circulated like a thin black cloud around and in between Doctor Tscharner and this girl. She brushed up the dead hair and threw it in the fire. She hoped the girl would get bald. But she didn't. The hair healed like the rest of her.

The girl looked at them and her eyes did not inquire. When he spoke to her, she looked straight back at him and replied in sparse words, volunteering nothing. Her pulse returned to normal, striking his fingers like a hard cord eighty times a minute. She did not like him to feel her pulse. He saw her distaste clearly pictured in her eyes though there was never an expression on her lips.

13

Jonah came to take her back at the end of July. "Pa can't pay nothin. She'll come work it off, ifen that's agreeable."

Doctor Tscharner agreed. He did not know what he would do with her, but he agreed. She came on foot through the woods, appearing suddenly at the clearings, as silent and accurate as a bird. Her feet were bare and often muddy, sometimes scratched, as if she had walked in brambles.

Doctor Tscharner did not like her coming. Pheny feared it. She clutched Tscharner's child to her bosom. Pheny looked upon this Cassandra as though she wore a mantle of contagion. She had wanted her master to take a woman, but a woman of quality, as the other had been. This one that came up from the river and walked on naked feet, this one that had been ill and exposed under his hand, who had vomited up from the bottom of her guts and let out her blood like milk out of an udder, this Cassandra Keith was a fearful thing.

He sent her to the forest to gather herbs. He was particular: gum, resin, roots, bark, berries, leaves, flowers; he told her precisely what he wanted. He charged her with the task and was curious to see if she could match it.

She knew that she was being put to the proof and it amused her in a strange new way. The weather was dry. The mist had been absorbed and the blank sky held no clouds. It was not the time for barks, she told him, tossing her hair. A strand of it caught on her cheek. Their time was either in spring, when it was resin he wanted, or in fall, for gum. In either case, she went on, it must be taken from young trees so that it might be stripped more easily and would be less decayed. She pulled back the strand of hair.

Her words were not correctly put, her syntax was confusing, but she made herself understood in an abrupt forceful way. Doctor Tscharner listened to her spare unadorned speech and he took the things she brought back. And he made no remarks in return.

Cassandra felt at first no enthusiasm at her task. She was relieved at its gentleness, though she knew she walked some kind of measuring stick before him. The plants of the forest, their times to appear and flourish, then drop off and die, their places of culture: these things she had known from her earliest years. No person had shown her, told her, taken her by the hand and pointed it out on a clear day in good weather. Her knowledge of the world was derived from her physical contact with it for seventeen years. And it was through this contact, harsh and sensible for the most part, though frequently serene and tinged with light, that she lost her identity in the things around her and was either soaked up in them or subtly enriched.

It was not for Doctor Tscharner that she learned these herbs and barks and seeds. It was because of him, however, that she came to learn that these things that sprang up in quietness and unclasped their leaves to molecules of infinite sunlight bore the secrets of healing. She became absorbed in the discovery, elevated, and at last thrilled through to the bone.

After the dew was off, she wandered through the trees and grubbed. Blacksnake root grew in rich woodlands. Its leaves were shaped like a heart and its flowers were of a purplish-brown intensity. She picked apart the roots that grew in clumps of strings matted together. They tasted bitter and made her pulse rise. Their aromatic smell clung to her fingers as she sorted out those that were spoiled, worm-eaten, and washed them with a small brush in the cold water of Apion creeks. They would dry immediately in the air. She spread them in the shade, turning them many times to expose every part.

Foxglove grew two feet tall, and for this she did not go to the woods, but to her own yard. She cultivated it because she liked its purple blossoms hanging down in a row like fingers. And inside, the finger blossoms were mottled all over with little spots that looked like little eyes. She stroked the row of purple fingers and they shivered. The little eyes bruised.

Cassandra pointed to a patch of earth near the surgery. "Can I have that?" she asked Ishmael. He shrugged his big shoulders, confused. "I reckon," he said, "you ast him first." She asked Doctor Tscharner. The bizarre request intrigued him and he replied, "Yes," before he had thought better of it.

She broke the earth and spaded it. She transplanted foxglove from the river to the mountain. She put papers over the plants to protect them from the sun until they took root. He did not count the days, but it was not many before a row of foxglove stood there with large egglike leaves.

He took the leaves when they were dry. He powdered them and put them into liquor. He rolled them into pills with soap or bread. He used her foxglove to abate rapid pulses, diminish circulation through consumptive lungs, stop bleeding at the nose, or to dry up excessive menstruation. He did not use the purple blossoms, the little mottled eyes.

Calamus she found down in the shallow places. Its long leaves glistened bright as swords. Water seeped through the earth under her feet as she pulled the calamus. It was late summer, past the season for green calamus that tasted sweet. But she searched it out and brought it, dried, in the manner of blacksnake root. Doctor Tscharner grated it into water for children who suffered colic. Or he mixed it with dogwood and cherry to stave off the pains of ague.

For hart's-tongue, Cassandra searched among rocky places, in the shade of the mountain, until she found the long shiny black leaves shaped like tongues. She tied them into bundles, throwing away those that were withered or blotched, and hung them from the walls of his plant shed. It was warm inside. The sun struck the many panes of glass in a huge golden wash. Ishmael raised and lowered the windows to change the currents of air that nurtured the tropical plants.

She was impressed by the sight of the glass, streaky, with tiny bubbles of air trapped in it, all of it polished and clean. She fingered the orange trees and measured the length of their green thorns. When her leaves were dry, Doctor Tscharner took a handful and simmered them in a pint of hog lard. He treated scalds, burns, lacerations.

She went to gather boneset immediately as the dew evaporated, seeking those freshest flowers which had opened that morning. Boneset flourished in wet places, in the meadows and marshes that lay near the river, on the damp shade-soaked embankments of the mountain creeks.

She picked the plant and held it up to her face. The stalk was hairy and tickled her like the legs of flies or the pink feathery cockades of the mimosa trees. The flowers, easily bruised and white, were attractive to insects. She disliked to find one crawling on the new flowers. With the tips of her fingernails, she flicked the insects away, twirling the stalk as she did. The rough dark-green leaves had tiny notches along their edges, like tiny green teeth. She peered closer and noticed how they were set, at right angles to one another, covered with fine hairs like the stalk.

Cassandra was pleased with boneset. The charms of this plant appealed to her. She brought it to him as fresh as she could and was careful not to expose its flowers to the sun or to bruise it. Boneset she dried, like hart's-tongue, in the warm delicate air of the shed, behind the golden lattice of the glass. And she was amazed at how much he used of it, at how thoroughly it gave itself to him.

He boiled it in water. Applied warm, it produced copious perspiration in his patients, making them throw off the poisons of their sickness. He powdered the dry leaves in the mortar until they were soft as dust and then administered them in syrups as gentle purgatives. And the white flowers, though bitter, were as strong in their healing as the flowers of camomile. They cured ringworm. And a wineglass full of the green juice of this same boneset that she found in the wet places of the forest could cure the stings of serpents. And its leaves, if bruised, could be applied to the wound.

She picked and grubbed, wandering over the mountain all day, wading in the brown bubbling water. She picked, discarded, sorted through, searched, and returned with her choices all stowed in a bundle, her nails ringed with dirt. And she did not waste words with Doctor Tscharner. She sat in the yard with the bundle opened at his feet and she dug the dirt out of her nails with a pine splinter. He examined her herbs. He observed how she went about cleaning them with water and the brush, how she peeled and sliced them and strung them on pieces of thread or tied them in bunches to hang and dry. Her products did not intrude in the shed. Her row of foxglove was complemented by rows of other herbs that adapted themselves to a tame garden: arrowroot, camomile, dill, fennel, senna, sage, thyme, and bee balm.

109

The space that she took up, she used to his advantage always. And she did not alter his dimensions one hair.

Cassandra Keith, in her place, observed this man with an uncanny penetration. She was artful in her untrained sense of perception. And she was unusual in that she understood what she saw, even in its darkest and most hidden places.

His child called Lieschen, standing under the fig bush that grew next to the chimney, was stung on her hand by some small red wasps. She did not cry. She frowned and rubbed her hand frantically against her stomach and called to her father. *"Vater! Vater!"*

Cassandra, who sat on the stoop of the surgery, witnessing, killed the wasps. Doctor Tscharner appeared in the door, and when he understood what had happened, he picked up the child and spoke to her in comforting tones, in a strange language. It annoyed Cassandra that he used the German. It annoyed her to feel closed out, though she knew perfectly she had not one claim for belonging. Still it annoyed her deeply to hear the unfamiliar sounds in his mouth and to hear the child reply.

She took notice how he spoke to the child, not as to a child, but as to another person possessing the same faculties of intelligence as himself. And she perceived immediately his pleasure in the child's indifference to pain. He did not like tears. The child did not cry, was not subdued by her injury.

Doctor Tscharner carried this Lieschen into the surgery and without any tender pandering display spread a liniment of hartshorn and oil over her hand and sent to the kitchen for fresh butter.

‡

It did not surprise Cassandra when later he took her into the surgery and set her to filling the glass bottles and helping dispense the medicines. It was appealing. The blue flame of the Bunsen, with its starkly nauseating smell, did not offend her. She helped him well. He allowed her to touch and look, to move freely, and though she would not ask him one thing, she would hesitate and proceed only at his direction. She did not clutter the air with useless energies. He let her read his books. Crust by crust, he fed her with the knowledge of diuretic infusion, anodynes, ointments and gargles and pills, poultices of pumpkin seeds, white sugar, lead, vitriol, spirits of niter. He measured them out to her in grains: twenty grains, a scruple, three scruples, a drachm, eight drachms, one ounce.

And when she had finished feeding on this bait, she sat looking at the surgery with wide grey eyes. She looked at the glass tubes in the rack, the stone mortar in which he pounded and rubbed the things she read about, the steel lancet in its leather, the rows of bottles she had filled, stacks of bandages torn from clean boiled rags, boiled and bleached in Pheny's black pot, the books that possessed a smell and touch and sound of whispering pages to tease her relentlessly. Lastly, she looked at the black cape hanging from a nail.

And when she felt Doctor Tscharner looking, she did not freeze as an animal freezes in the brush to escape his hunter. She barely stiffened, draining her eyes of their uncommon interests.

14

The debt had been paid. Still she came. And he could not control it. She swelled through him like turgor. The tensions disobeyed him, tightened, tumulted, and released sharp currents at the sight of her skirt flapping against her bare legs. She came up the slope. There was nothing beautiful about her face. She laid down the herbs. Her silence was persistent, yet she arranged her herbs with the sharpest articulation. Her mind was not sealed. And her eyes, grey and elusive, absorbed him, infected him, and he could not be absolved.

Cassandra Keith was a small, lean thing. The muscles in her were hard and the bottoms of her feet were stained from the dust and mineral water. She spread out the herbs in the shade of the acacia trees, turning them over, picking out those that were shriveled, studying each particle. She squatted over them and remained squatting for long periods of time, her lithe joints impervious to fatigue.

Rutha and Pheny spied on her from the kitchen. "Looky yonder at 'er," snorted Rutha, stirring a bowl of batter in the crook of her arm. "She could squat and pick and singe a whole chicken!"

Pheny squinted out the door. She looked like a mole emerging from its burrow, the sudden brilliance striking its bad eyes. "Ain't no raising in 'er. She ain't had no raising. She knows herself she ain't had no raising."

Rutha poured the batter in a deep black pan and shoved it in the oven. She returned to the window. "Still out yonder squattin! She burned plumb black as me!"

"Ain't no raising," echoed Pheny, "ain't no raising at all."

The sun had darkened her arms. And her plain brown-colored hair rushed down the middle of her back, thick and straight. She had been raised without beauty. The only delicate feature of Cassandra Keith was the pale scar that lay like a tiny crescent moon below her eye.

Doctor Tscharner became indifferent to buxom beauty, full and bubbling, the robust red-cheeked kinds. He saw white mist evaporating before his hands, a foam of the sea that smelled faintly rotten and left a damp salty taste. He felt the membranes of bursting bubbles. He came upon spider webs lain everywhere across bushes and grass, sparkling in their chains of dew, vibrating at the touch of his foot and wrecking completely beyond repair.

Aaron Bloodworth came to ask advice about his children, who, he reported, suffered with worms. He stared at the girl standing barefooted in the surgery. He noticed how she was spoken to by Doctor Tscharner, how she moved among the medicines, how her presence (which to him seemed so rare and extraordinary) was to Tscharner a smooth, well-oiled part of his existence.

He described his children. "They scratch at their tail all day and grind their teeth all night. And what time they aren't engaged in these two occupations, they are picking at their noses, coughing, and whining." Bloodworth grimaced and drummed his fingers on the table. His eyes contoured the girl.

"What have you done for them?" asked Doctor Tscharner. He was displeased at Bloodworth's unabashed scrutiny of Cassandra Keith. He began to feel he was responsible for something that he could not discern. The feeling annoyed him. An immodest anger suffused his blood. "Well?" he pressed.

Bloodworth transferred his scrutiny to the doctor. He smiled knowingly. "I gave 'em a good dose of calomel. I got 'em cleaned out."

Doctor Tscharner's anger took root and blossomed. "You are aware that I discourage the intemperate use of calomel, Master Bloodworth?" He crashed his fist on the table between them and was immediately shocked by his lack of restraint. He gestured with exasperation. "The element mercury is a strong poison. It purges, it heals, but it can also leave the body with such damage that in the end the use of it is perhaps more injurious than beneficial."

He stood up and went to the shelves. He stood for a moment, collecting his reason, then said firmly, "No more calomel, I beg of you, if you wish to save your children from blindness, rheumatisms, stomach irritations, even death." He took down a bottle of iron filings.

"The task at hand is to exterminate the vermin, if indeed they do exist within the bowels of your children. I am inclined to believe in most cases they are more suspected than real."

The words came as though from a textbook. Doctor Tscharner had said a great deal. And he was aware of having made a great fool of himself, not only over the calomel, but also over the invisible trial that he and the girl had stood in the eyes of Aaron Bloodworth.

He passed into the small anteroom that adjoined the surgery. It was a room where he kept patients, the room where he had kept Cassandra Keith for the duration of her malignant fever. Now it was empty and she had stored bunches of roots there. He took some that were called pinkroot. She looked at the blush on his face. It was the first time she had ever seen him agitated. And she realized that she must have had something to do with it.

He returned to Bloodworth, folding a small rag around the roots. "Tell your wife to boil a handful of this pinkroot in water, perhaps a quart, and give them a cupful each evening and in the morning before they have had anything to eat. You may flavor it with milk and sugar, if they desire. But you must watch for any redness in their eyes. If they should complain of any soreness, cease the cure at once. So much for pinkroot."

He tapped the filings on a piece of paper and creased it with precision, the corners sharp, like arrows. "To avoid a new growth," he said quietly, the blush fading from his face, "forbid them all greasy foods for at least one month. And give them this tonic several times a day. No more than a pinch of snuff, mixed in well with molasses."

Aaron Bloodworth took the packet of iron filings and the pinkroot and, with one back look at the girl who entered like a shadow from the anteroom, rode home. When he got to the mill, he was beside himself with curiosity. He shouted at the Negroes to adjust the gate, to increase the turn of the wheel, to sweep and flap at the flies. He worked them like the slaves of Egypt and all the while he burned to know Tscharner's secret. He sat on the porch and thought about it all the rest of the week. It galled him that he could be so curious. It became his sore spot, and at times he was angry with Doctor Tscharner, at other times he was disgusted.

"She's a good girl," he argued with himself out loud, "but she ain't never knowd nothing. Excepting hard work. And that brother of hers would cut somebody's liver out and make 'em look at it!"

"Ooh!" squealed Hannah, then scolded him, "Don't meddle."

"I ain't!" he retorted. But the following week, when Doctor Tscharner came and looked at the children, he could not keep from blurting, "That little Keith, she ain't for you. Ain't your kind. Too common. A common pa. Common brother. No good, Shanner. Don't you see that?"

Doctor Tscharner glanced up slowly from the small girl he was examining. She had pinkish freckles and the tip of her nose had peeled from sunburn. He did not reply to Bloodworth's arguments. He let them hang in the air like a cloud. He rode away.

He came back late in August, one evening when everything was approaching a heavy ripening and the summer drought had lasted many weeks. He sat with Aaron Bloodworth on the mill porch and they both listened to the pallid washing of low water against the dam.

Tscharner lit his pipe. The ember glowed in his eyes. His black eyes were without innocence, black and full to their brim. Bloodworth lifted the demijohn. He strangled and coughed, inhaling the corn liquor. Tears ran down his face. "Goddamn it!" He spat into the dark yard. The dogs sniffed at his spittle, then continued to plunder through the bushes. They sat down and scratched at their fleas, twisting their necks tortuously to get at those on their backs. The dogs panted with the heat. They yawned.

Doctor Tscharner smoked a long time in silence; there was only the gentle wheezing of his pipe, the puckering sound of his lips around the stem. The long dark warm glowing evening passed into night. The dogs slept at Bloodworth's feet, twitching, groaning. Doctor Tscharner got up and knocked the ash from his pipe. He held out his hands to Bloodworth.

"Look at my hands," he ordered. Bloodworth looked. The palms were down, the knuckles were white as moonseed vines, each nail opaque. "I am strong in my hands, Bloodworth."

He rode off into the blackness. The dogs got up and barked at him. The horse's hoofs thudded in the dust. Aaron Bloodworth remained looking dumbly into the night, puzzling what had just happened. Above him the seven flares of the Dipper burned. The thready Pleiades twinkled virulently and he could not look directly at them, but only out of the corner of his eye. As the echo of Doctor Tscharner was absorbed by the black air, he spoke to himself gently and reassuringly, "He's crazy as a bedbug, ain't he? And it's his own fault, too."

Aaron Bloodworth went to bed and dreamed. He held out his hand and opened it and a toy Cassandra Keith stood there on the hard white calluses. Her eyes glinted like grey-colored glass. Doctor Tscharner spoke to him from somewhere, but every time he turned toward the voice, it moved away, and he could only hear it out of the corner of his eye. "I am stronger. Don't you see that?"

And while Aaron Bloodworth watched, stupefied, through his dreaming brain, Doctor Tscharner struck off his hand at the wrist and the toy exhaled into ash.

Over eight miles away, Cassandra Keith waked in her bed and looked at the dark ugly ceiling. The wind had risen and thunder disturbed the stillness. She sat up. For an instant, the moon, like a lamp turned full-beam into her face, broke through a moil of greyish clouds and illumined the panes of the window. The glass was greasy, fretted with fingerprints, and the dried bodies of insects stuck to the corners.

She slid out of bed and went to the window and, raising the sash, peered out. At the far end of the yard the dust of the Kelly Star Road spread in a gleaming band down to the river and along the dark embankment. Down this road came a man and a horse. As they passed the gate, Cassandra drew in her breath. The sound of the black hoofs hammering the gleaming road attacked her ears with the pulsations of her own blood.

"Don't he never rest?" she marveled. Thunder shook the sill under her arms and rain began to spatter in the dust.

15

He thought he would have stopped it. Just as he would have stopped the plunge of the temperature, the moon phases, the flight of wild geese in the autumn. But the loneliness beat down upon him its terrible wings and he lost his command. The clamming rain stuck along the collar of his black bombazine. The wind shrieked. He found himself before an unkind mirror of high polish. He had come in search of room. Jeanne-Catherine Pons had died. The room, the great enormous space he sought after, had never been revealed to her. Because of this, she had been brought to mud and rock and the humiliating misery of an old man shucking corn in a drizzle of rain.

He would have stopped all of it and trapped it inside a single tear of amber, put it to sleep, suspended. But the roaring of the Great Falls drowned him out. The water crashed over the rocks, foaming yellow and white, and purged the bowels of the river.

The changing of the moon and the opening up of the earth beneath his feet made him a liar. Everything went on as though nothing had happened. The world took no notice of him. Locusts fell and split open and lay drying in the sun. Their shiny brown skins crunched under his boot. In spring jonquils had spread through the grass, yellow and unstained. His house was soon ringed round in swelling myrtle trees and his plum thickets frothed against the dark cedars. Summer appeared. His body sweated. At night, southern constellations stung the sky with white, irreligious, pure, and uncaring stars.

Doctor Tscharner walked in these nights. He rode. He was a somnambulist, and the horse took on the silence of a fish in deep water. When the moon came up, it was white and stood over the dark peaks of the mountain and cast long white beams down the trees. He saw how the trees and the house and the horse he sat upon made shadows on the ground. They cast shadows as though the hour were noon. The ground was bright and the river dazzled. The spaces between the trees were black and deep as cellar holes. Deer, feeding in the meadows, jerked up their heads at his approach and the moon flashed from their eyes. He rode through the bright forest quietly, keeping the horse to a walk, slowly, absorbing the moon and the darkness, advancing always to the river.

He came out on a cliff. Rhododendron clustered to the very edge of it and spilled over. He looked down at the river and the house of the ferryman. The roof gleamed like glass. The ferryboat, tied to the dock, undulated milky lights. Across the narrow river, the forest of Weymouth showed blue-green in the intense moon.

The horse stamped and neighed. Doctor Tscharner sat still and looked at the river and the house and the moon over all. He noticed the rough escarpments on the face of the moon. They stood out plainly, as plainly as the pocks on the face of a man. Mosquitoes came out of the rhododendron and stung his body. Crickets and toads shrieked irksomely. He heard the steady pouring of water over the Falls upriver. The moon moved to the west in imperceptible degrees.

He became aware of a movement. A white figure appeared. Its face and limbs were dark, but its body reflected the rays of the moon as freely as a patch of new snow. It moved lissomely across the white dirt, bending easily, and then faded into the trees at the river.

He spoke to the horse, scarcely moving his lips to make the sounds, and they moved down. The rhododendron rustled, opening up and then closing behind the horse, sealing itself in shadows.

It grew worse for him. Lieschen became foreign. She was a stranger's child, dandled in Pheny's arms, fed from a spoon by slaves, a small incoherent girl for whom he often felt an evanescent remorse. He tried to dream of his wife, but he had no more pictures of her. Her murder was complete. He spoke to Pheny. "We must stop it now. No use, now, for her to come here. I shall see to it this day." And Pheny looked at him curiously. He thought, "Can't she see how I am resisting it? What a torture it is to me? How I am abstaining from it?" Pheny kept looking at him, and when he saw the savage wisdom in her eyes, he cursed at her in his German. She sulked over her cooking.

There was scrofula at Wharftown. Keith ferried Doctor Tscharner and Cassandra over the river. He said nothing to his girl. But he looked at the doctor with the same naked wisdom that Pheny had used. Doctor Tscharner resisted doggedly. "The river is low," he remarked.

"I don't need morn a inch to float," answered the old man. His neck was like leather, a deep sunburned color, and grey hairs grew out of his nostrils. He jabbed at the water with a long pole. The current in midstream still carried the boat, but its shallowness on either shore forced him to pole in to the docks. He threw the rope around a piling. The piling was muddy, covered with blisters of dried algae. Doctor Tscharner led the horse ashore and turned to give his hand to the girl. But she evaded him by jumping to the dock. There was no one waiting, so Keith pushed off again.

They rode to Wharftown to a family called Threadgill. Their house was large, two stories, with a cupola. But the boards had warped. Black noisy starlings nested in the chimneys. A baby sat in the door, rubbing a piece of bread on the floor. Flies crawled around his bald head. His brothers and sisters were afflicted with scrofula, king's evil. Their mother, holding a bolt of cloth in her arm, ushered Doctor Tscharner and the girl into the sickroom. "They generally sleep upstairs, but it's been so hot, I moved 'em all down here."

The children lay in beds, some together in the same bed, and they were restless. They wanted to get up, to go out. "It ain't the first time," said the woman, "but it's the worst it's ever been."

Doctor Tscharner moved among the children. He felt the hard tumors behind their necks, ears, and under their chins. Lips and nostrils were swollen, the shiny skin stretched smooth. The softer tumors, on the verge of suppurating, were purple or reddish-colored. The children looked at him like hungry little birds, holding open their mouths to catch breath.

"Cantybelle. Maida. Rafe. De Witt. Ernest." The woman stopped at each bed, holding out her fingers to count. "It takes me awhile to think 'em all up," she explained. She turned with a frown. "And that's Lynn." The bald-headed baby had crawled into the room. His bread was grey from the floor and little black ants were entrenched in it.

"I put plasters on them sores," she continued, "to try to make 'em fester up and bust for the pus to get out. I figured that pus was the evil in it. Huh?"

"No, no." Doctor Tscharner shook his head sternly. "Suppuration must be avoided if possible. Warm plasters are wrong. You have done wrong. Cold water alone would have been of great benefit. If it has happened before, you should have known this. Why haven't you sought me before? Why don't you know these things?" He threw up his hands at her and glared.

She clutched her bolt of cloth and replied, "Well, I don't know. Maybe I think you supposed to use your common sense with your own child." She stuck out her lips and pouted.

Doctor Tscharner looked at the pouting, fishlike lips. He looked at the flies crawling on the baby. The baby's eyes seemed as mashed and deeply entrenched in the baldness of his skull as the mangled ants were in his piece of bread. "Common sense?" he said. "What is that?"

They bathed the children with cold water in which they had poured a pound of salt. They wiped away the pus from the broken ulcers and applied powdered bark and vinegar, covering these and the hard ones with brown paper and cold wet rags. "You must do this everyday," he told the woman, "to every child, to every tumor, uncover it and wash it and replace the brown paper with fresh."

She sulked over her cloth, measuring it out in the yard lengths by holding a stretch from her nose to the end of her fingers. "Yeh," she mumbled.

"And a drink of salted water with blacksnake root *each* morning. To *each* one." He insisted that she listen to him. She threw down the cloth and clamped both hands on her hips. "Yeh! Yeh!"

He was disgusted with it all, with the treatment, with the bald baby and his filthy bread, with the woman from whom the children no doubt had received scrofula in the natal plasma. Cassandra said hardly anything, a few soft words, a string of dim replies.

They crossed back. Keith hunched on the gunwales and watched the water sliding under the bow. "You got anything cooked up?" he asked the girl. It was noon and the sun stood directly overhead. Doctor Tscharner looked at the sun and then across the river. Black discs repeated themselves into infinity, bounced about by the bright water.

"I cooked up enough this morning to last you all day," she replied. "There's some squash and pone under the cloth. And some jack pie in a dish."

He set them ashore. The keel bumped in the mud. The girl left Doctor Tscharner without a word to go to the house. And when he returned to Apion, still feeling the form of her flesh clinging to his back, undulating with the surge of the horse, Pheny met him at the door and said severely, "Doctor Shanner, you is a foolsome man."

"What?" he snapped, uncomprehending. Then realizing, he agreed with her, appalled at what she had said and at what he had allowed, "a fool."

In the afternoon, he rode through Apion and he saw a sentinel crow in the top of a pine. The black creature spied him and flapped its wings and cawed. It did not fly, but remained in the top of the tree, keeping eye on the man below. The others, hearing the alarum, rose up in a loud cawing blackness from a meadow several yards away. The sight took on special meanings for him. He had rarely seen a bird making its call. Whippoorwills, flickers, thrushes, mourning doves: these he had seen, had heard making their calls, but never at the same time. Never had he been able to point to a bird and say, "There is a dove calling. I hear it. I see it." It was rare.

Doctor Tscharner returned home and went to bed. But he lay listening for birds. It was unusual to hear them at night. He had never heard a bird call in the night and he had long been a creature of darkness. He listened. He strained his ears. The birds were roosting. There was not one who waked and uttered his call.

He lay and the thoughts of Cassandra rolled down like a sea. She was as elusive as the birds. He was bigger and stronger; he was older. But she was more agile. She could outmaneuver him. For this girl, this Magdalene, he felt a homesickness, an emptiness in the bottom of his stomach. He felt he could weep with vexation.

His wife had been as an icon to him, a consort of perfect complement, correct. He would never have gone to her with these new hungers. The thoughts scalded him. He put up his hands and felt his burning cheeks and was shamed. He had skillfully ignored the blushing of his patients, the girls who cowered at his probing, the women who feared his exposures as much as they feared the throes of labor and who in the end begged as earnestly for the sheet as for laudanum. Now he, too, shared something of the same panic.

She was a Cleopatra, a Magdalene. She exposed. This Cassandra, who did not blush at nakedness or recoil from the touch of it, contradicted all he had been taught to expect from women. Her virginity shocked him beyond all else. And with it, he fell into a lime pit that went unslaked by water and suffered its heat to mount invisibly toward a dangerous degree.

16

She was attracted to the nightshades. Doctor Tscharner knew only one, the one in his book, and he told her its name in Latin, *Atropa belladonna*. She knew others, the bitter-sweet, the pokeberry, and the deadly nightshade. Her ma had lumped all of them under one name: pokeberry.

It grew on the piles of garbage in the yard, taking good healthy root in the chicken entrails her ma used to fling out the door. The round berries would change three times in their uncanny season, from green to red to a shining black. She ate them once on a dare and then puked her insides out all over the bushes, spattering her feet.

Her brothers laughed. She lay down in the dirt and heaved. She was so sick she couldn't curse. Her ma sat on the porch suckling a baby. The brothers laughed. They gathered around Cassie and grinned at her misery. She noticed with distaste that their freckles were milky-colored and their dirty hair was tangled and curled like a sheep's and grew way down their necks in whitish fuzz, soft as snuff. Her ma leaned over the edge of the porch. The baby lost his hold on her teat and sucked the empty air.

"Them pokeberries'll kill you," said her ma.

Cassandra rolled in the dirt. Her dress yellowed with it and the corners of her mouth turned purplish from the vomit. She rolled to the edge of the woods and lay panting, her eyes fixed on the green boughs swelling above her. "Ain't gonna kill me, you old bitch," she muttered. "Ain't!"

Now she gathered pokeberries, the black nightshade, for Doctor Tscharner. She found it in waste places, in piles of rubbish, old pastures, old fields grown up with briers. All of the nightshade was poison. That intrigued her. With its awkward leaves that stretched on stems as much as eight feet into the air, its white flowers that appeared in July, its dark berries shining with a high polish, and its fleshy taproot, *Atropa belladonna* was suffused with peril. The berries hung in clusters like grapes. She picked them and burst them open in her palm. The juice glistened.

This was a deadly thing. But in his hands, it performed wonders. It cured palsy, jaundice, dropsy, and dried up the sores of scirrhus. But it was constantly dangerous. He began with small doses, half a grain of the powdered leaves boiled in a pint of water, strained through a sieve. This was as much as he allowed an adult in the beginning of his cure. He gradually increased it, but when any strange symptom appeared, no matter how slight, he suspended the belladonna immediately and waited until it had passed. Thus, Doctor Tscharner made medicine of poison, broke the nightshade to his will, and cured with it.

The one called bittersweet she found growing over other bushes and climbing along ditches. This one was not as virulent as the other. Its winding stalks were clustered with blue flowers that shrank from the sun and withered quickly. The berries were red and they tasted at first sweet, then grew bitter. She would not take any berries that had fallen to the ground. She gathered handfuls of the twigs and leaves, peeled the roots, and brought them to him. He steeped them in wine or vinegar, adding flaxseeds.

She watched Doctor Tscharner prepare nightshade, deadly belladonna, bittersweet, and she said recklessly, all of a sudden, "Listen, I heard my ma tell about poke sallet onct. Poke sallet's good, you know, for the liver, but you got to get it just right, when it's still green, just starting to shoot up, early. If you get it too old, it'll kill you. And even that early sallet's deadly if you ain't got enough grease."

She put her hands on her hips and with one bare toe began fidgeting over the rough plank floor. She had trimmed off her toenails square across the ends. "Ma knew of some folks that gathered poke sallet one spring and didn't have no hawg meat. They went ahead and boiled up a potful and eat it and it killed every last one of 'em!"

She stopped and drew in her breath, ashamed. She had run off at the mouth. Her voice had rent the quiet air between them. The sounds of what she had said clattered down and lay on the planks at her feet. She kicked at the floor and went away. She wanted to look back to see if he was laughing at her, but she couldn't.

She went home. Boone was there, sitting on the top step, scratching at the mosquito bites on his legs. "Whar you been?" he said. "I'm hongry."

"Shut up," she replied, and went in the house. Shortly, she came back with a dish of clabber and a chunk of pone. She gave him a spoon and he began to eat the clots of sour milk, dipping the pone in the dish and sucking it. "It's real good, Cassie," he grunted.

"Yes," she agreed, pleased by his relish, "good." She went to the kitchen and laid out food for Jonah and her pa. The came and ate and wandered away again. Jonah kept talking about finding his vein of gold and getting gone from all of them for good. Her pa scoffed at him. "Ain't no gold in that clay! Ain't nothing but red worms and cow shit!"

They went over the river to Weymouth. It grew dark. Cassandra took Boone into the kitchen and washed him from a pan. He complained, "You going get soap in my eyes! You going get it in my sores! Don't! It going hurt! Oh, don't you *hear* it?" He squirmed under her rag. She pulled his nightdress off the nail and forced his head through it. They went upstairs. She pulled the truckle bed out from under her own. Boone went to sleep and she lay on the hot sheet looking at him. She held out her hands before her in the dark. They looked very white and clean, shriveled like peanut hulls from the water. Boone began to snore. The others were gone to Weymouth. Maybe Jonah was finding his vein. They paid no mind to her.

She got up and went to the window. She pulled the sacking over the window so that the moon, when it rose, would not shine in Boone's eyes and awaken him. Then she went down the stairs, soundless as a cat.

Deception became easy to them and took on a weird dreamlike logic. She got up in the morning and milked the cow, brought butter from the spring for breakfast, and cooked up enough food to last all day. She left Boone or let him tag behind her as she rambled the woods for Doctor Tscharner.

And Doctor Tscharner sat at his famous table, served by his slaves. It was easy, he found, to be wise and stern, frowning at the patients, poking their hollow bellies, gouging the yellow wax from their ears. The daylight made it very easy. He employed the steel lancet. He rode through the forest purging and bleeding, granting delivery from death and also from life. Doctor Philip Tscharner had come into this land to heal by the laying on of hands and shrewdness of his nature. He had absolved himself. He no longer felt craven, as though he were choking on sea water or the fumes of camphor, upbraiding himself for his emotional disorder. He had found a prevailing rhythm of unusual cadence that flowed around him and made him impervious to shame or guilt.

And at night, while his stern, glittering, clean day-self lay still, sleeping like death, like a heavy sickness, he rode off to her by the river. The water bubbled over clear grey granite, high above the sluggish Council. This was the water of the Great Falls, where a pine log, thrown in, would have its bark beaten off smooth in seconds. The water poured barbarously, squandering the moisture of the uplands. Down below, it sank into the clay, was sucked up in mud and drained to a shallow ooze. But here the thick moss exuded a fertile smell and the mushrooms were broad as a man's hand.

She was there, appearing like a shadow from behind the trees, wading carelessly in the foaming circles of water that spilled off from the Falls and lay in shallow pools at the edge of the trees. They could not speak against the sound of the Falls. They could only think and their thoughts screamed. But once she whispered, to his joy, pushing her hands rudely against his face and pressing her lips to his ear, "I wisht I had you in a bottle. I'd stop you up so tight you couldn't *breathe!*"

Then she laughed and, as she took her hands down, fireflies glittered in the dark air, delicate as eyelids. Their little jabbing fires thrummed over the water and were extinguished in the spray.

"Look," she commanded in a hoarse whisper. He turned toward the sound. She was thin and luminescent, like a film of naked fireflies.

He seemed to bloom at night. He was nocturnal. He stayed in the night so long he forgot that it was night, that the air was black, that the Falls pounded on perilous rock. The rhythm took hold of him and dragged him round and round.

Then, at the deepest, ripest part of the season, with the

night creatures crying and the stars blistering the sky with a brilliance of the first magnitude, Doctor Tscharner rode to the river and she was not there.

He waited. The Falls poured over the rock, throwing spray against the leaves, flashing through the brambles and making his face cold. Doves cried out in the dark recesses of the woods and he did not notice. The racket of the insects became tedious and more powerful than the roar of the water.

It was unbelievable to him, unreal, that he could find himself sweating on the dark moss, alone and unanswered. He grew sullen and mounted the horse. On Apion, the smell of summer was everywhere, heavy and hopelessly with child. He went into the empty surgery and blew out all the lamps and fell on the bed.

17

The big fish glided. He tapered his blue fins and turned abruptly, disturbing the algae. Cassandra lay on her side, one-half of her body submerged in the river, her nightdress bellying with the current. She reached out for the fish. He swam obediently toward the white weaving fingers. The dull-black bead of his eyeball rotated in gleaming water and his cold lip nursed at the hem of her dress. Then, as he was within one curl of her finger, he swerved again and was gone, leaving behind a long chain of bubbles.

The bedstead creaked under her and she woke up. The night outside was festooned with fireflies. Down the road, miles away, she could hear the horse coming. Doctor Tscharner's horse coming down the dark.

The snoring of her little brother brought her back to life and she wiped the sweat from her face with the tail of the nightdress. "I dreamed a fish," she murmured, then addressed the room, "I dreamed a fish."

Boone whined in his sleep and turned. Outdoors, through all the river groves and low-lying places, bullfrogs bellowed. They thumped and swelled relentlessly, pulling at the darkness as if it were a heavy black udder. The groves were ablaze with tiny lights, the bodies of insects, and the creeping phosphorescence of the mist. "How did I dare?"

She thought of him waiting unrequited at the Falls. And she did not feel anything. She only marveled at herself again. "How did I dare?"

She jerked up the nightdress and peered at her body. "Ain't much," she calculated. Frowning, she plucked at a nipple with her thumb and forefinger. It was hard. A drop glistened. It trickled slowly around her pressing thumb and fell down. She felt dizzy. She dropped back on the bed, throwing up her arms to bring more darkness.

The moon had risen. It was not full, but in its third quarter. Still it shone with an uncanny luster and flooded the world. Boone sat up in the truckle bed and whispered, "Cassie, Cassie?"

"Lay down," she hissed, "hush."

"Lemme get in bed with you," he said.

She moved over as he climbed in beside her. "Tickle me," he ordered and turned on his side. Cassandra pulled up his dress. His small buttocks were white against the dark of his legs. She began to skim her fingers over his ribs and vertebrae. He fell asleep and snored. She withdrew her hand and lay still, curled, gazing over Boone at the window. She couldn't see the moon. It stood too far west over the roof. But the chalky moonbeams filled the room and wallowed across her bed.

She closed her eyes and began to think. She thought of Doctor Tscharner, big and tall, with black eyes, hard as black rocks. In the moonlight, his skin had been white and the muscles of his arms fastened around her like bands of white steel. She marveled at how she could have been swept up in that power. The chalk-colored cold steel that she liked and welcomed and encouraged and helped to fasten around herself was, nevertheless, after the moon had died and the morning come back, always chalk-colored and cold and ruthless as steel. His eyes pierced through her like nails. He confused her, adorned her, dazzled her, and left her feeling half-fed, perplexed, unable to make up her mind.

And she realized, without glee or pride, that should any other man, one of her brothers, her pa, any man that lived in Larkin County, should any one of them dare to touch her the way that Doctor Tscharner did, she would vomit in his face and pull out his eyeballs with her fingers.

She wanted to get into his eyes. She wanted to take him all apart and lay the pieces out and look at them, especially his eyes. Doctor Tscharner's eyes existed in the face of his child. Whenever she came to Apion, there would be Lieschen standing in the yard with a fig in her fist or sitting in a small cart that was hitched to a pony. And she would look at Cassandra with the same piercing black eyes. "Lizzie," she mumbled.

Boone twitched his feet against her belly and she opened

her eyes and looked. "He ain't much moren a baby," she thought, comparing him to Lieschen. She tried to recollect exactly when her ma had died. Boone must be seven or eight, she figured, still confused by her dreams and her half-sleep, her indecision wrought by Doctor Tscharner. Boone did not remember their ma. He did not remember being nursed on her bulging teat. Cassandra smiled wryly. She remembered too much, about all of them. The day her ma had weaned Boone reared up in her memory, silly and raw and violent.

He was big enough to walk and he had bitten her. She explained it to Cassie as she blackened herself with soot from the fireplace and pulled hairs from her head and stuck them on the nipple. Then she sat down in the chair. It was not long before Boone ran in. "Ninny-ma, ninny-ma," he demanded. Calmly she opened her dress and drew it out. He gaped at the black teat, filthy with hairs. He stepped backward. "Kill it! Kill it!" he yelled. "Get Pa's gun and shoot it!" And he pointed to the rifle over the door. He ran away. And he was weaned.

Cassandra giggled in her sleep. The moon sank lower and took back all its white light. The world grew dim and greenish with the dawn.

The summer passed. September came to the mountain, scattering a redness over the river, splotching the leaves, smelling like smoke. Now Cassandra Keith went to the gum trees, acacia, mimosa, the tall evergreen camphor tree. She stripped their bark and Doctor Tscharner took it and distilled it into arabic and camphor. He mixed it with wax or put it into bottles. She did not like the bark of the prickly ash. It was covered with prickles, and when she chewed a strip, it tasted hot, acrid, making her have to spit and salivate copiously. Doctor Tscharner boiled this bark in water or steeped the ash berries in alcohol. Such elixir was good for rheumatism and colic. And he recommended chewing the hot bark to relieve the twinges of a toothache.

The red season disappeared. Dry corn stood in shocks and pumpkins swelled in the fields, hard and yellow. The mornings were full of white mist and the twilight came down in a blue haze, echoing with bird calls. When it rained now there was no thunder or lightning, just the hard thud of the raindrops beating on roof and tree. The anemic river replenished itself with the hard grey-colored rain and Aaron Bloodworth's wheel turned again. Cassandra Keith counted through three moons and her suspicions were correct. She was pregnant. She kept it to herself, walled up, and she drew a strange comfort from its immunity. Doctor Tscharner read the signs. But to speak of it would cause great damage.

She did not know how to be vulnerable, or defenseless, so she became hostile. Her hostility crowded out her fear and her grief. It propped her up and made her proud. She looked with an even greater distaste upon her pa. She refused to tell him anything. She walked in her own world, immune, sealed off, hostile, uncaring.

In October, old Keith sent Jonah to tend to the interesting business involving Doctor Tscharner and his girl, Cassandra. Jonah fired one shot, straight up into the air. Doctor Tscharner came from the surgery. Ishmael and Clegg ran up from the barn and Pheny appeared in the door of the kitchen, holding Lieschen by a hand. Cassandra looked up from the bundle of roots she was washing in a bucket. Jonah spat tobacco and motioned toward her. "What you going do about that big belly?"

"Go away, you sorry fool," she said, turning her back on him. He spat again. "What you going do about it?" he asked Doctor Tscharner.

Doctor Tscharner did not answer. He looked at the girl bent over the bucket. It was true. He had been a fool. She would not look at him. Her fingers pulled apart the muddy fibers and rinsed them in the bucket. She stripped the withered leaves and pinched off decayed parts. Her hands glistened. Water splashed, making the hem of her skirt dirty. She straightened and wiped her hands on her apron and his gaze fell upon the new swelling in her breasts, the thrusting forth of her belly. He had not taken it seriously. He had not permitted himself to believe in it. That it was so, that it truly existed and took up space in her flesh, now became stridently manifested.

Jonah twisted in the saddle and grinned. "Well?" he prodded. "Pa's wondering." He put the gun across his shoulder and tipped his head back in a deep roll of laughter.

It was then she ran toward him and struck the horse with a switch. "Go to hell, Jonah," she shouted, "get out of here!" The horse charged away with the startled Jonah clinging to his back.

She picked up the gun from where it had fallen and fired after her brother. He was gone. The shot whistled through the air, slicing off dry leaves, and sank.

She gave the gun to Doctor Tscharner without a word and returned to the roots. He noticed his slaves standing white-eyed and he shouted at them hoarsely, "Well! What has possessed the lot of you? Have you nothing to do but stand and gape at us?"

They dispersed and he went inside the surgery. He laid the gun across the table and he was dismayed to find that his hands were trembling. He sat down and held them out before his eyes. The fingertips twitched. He felt his heart thumping against his ribs and he was hideously angered. He crashed his fist upon the table and swore in German.

She brought in the bunch of roots and stood with them, cleanly scraped, in her apron. She did not speak. He reached out his hands again and said to her, "Do you see?" She gazed at them, at the trembling fingers, long and white, and she replied, "Yes." There was no pity in the sound.

He crashed them on the table again and swore at her. She narrowed her eyes and dumped the roots on the table beside the gun. She turned away from him and went to stand in front of the fireplace. A pile of charred logs lay blanketed with thin ashes. There had been no new fire laid this morning. There had been no patients. A bad odor came from the dead hearth. She stood like a statue and refused to let him see her.

He scrutinized her. Her hair was long and stubbornly straight. It was washed clean and it was unadorned. The weight of it seemed to pull her head back and slant the corners of her eyes. Aaron Bloodworth had told him once, when discoursing on the gifts of women, "My ma had hair so long that when she sat in a chair and let it hang, it hung down and touched the floor!" He seemed triumphant, proud of it, his mother's long hair touching the floor. Doctor

Tscharner had thought it no virtue, only a circumstance. It was now no virtue, but a circumstance that brought this stubborn elusive girl, Cassandra, to stand before him hostile, tantalizing, puffed up with pride, condemning. The terrible childishness of the universe blossomed in his brain.

He could not allow it. He got up and turned her around, pressing her shoulders with his fingers, and said between tightly clenched teeth, "If ever you turn from me, I will kill you." Taking the gun, he went across the yard and into his house. The latch fell into place.

She remained all day in the surgery in front of the dead fire. She poked in the feathery ashes, whacked the black logs with the poker, and when she had done all she knew to keep off the tears, she had to relent and pull her apron over her face and weep. The simple pieces of the design were gone. A way of life had approached its end and she was faced with the new one that offered itself. The hostility within her was giving way. She wanted to annihilate them, castrate them, strike them off. It scalded her to think of Jonah coming to Apion. It shamed her. And when she had finished crying, she took hold of herself and peeled off the bad parts. These parts she buried in the grey ashes, under the black logs, the bad smell, the sour smell.

No patients came all day. For that she was exceedingly glad. She sat on the hearth and inhaled the odor of the burned logs, the oily soot. She listened to the wind whine through the chimney hole. It ruffled the soot on the stones. She had nothing but the clothes on her back and one cold chunk of pone in her apron. She chewed like a dog at the pone, without tasting, and swallowed.

In the late hours, he sent Rutha to bring her into the house. She stood on the parlor rug. It felt cold beneath her feet and the hard braided strips protruded and made her stumble. Evening was falling rapidly. He ordered a fire laid in the room to knock the chill. And when Clegg had gone, he said to Cassandra Keith, "I am what you might call an honorable man." Then he, too, left her. She heard the horse gallop past. The new fire blazed orange and scarlet in front of her and she felt her face getting warm, though her hands remained cold and her bare feet ached. Her time, her senses were quite distorted. She could not comprehend how much later or sooner it was when Doctor Tscharner came back. He brought two men into the house with him, the miller Aaron Bloodworth and Lentz, the preacher from Rocky Run.

"How foolish this all is," she thought, "how crazy." Her face burned as bright as the fire. It was black night outside and the glass in the windows was slick with the blackness. It reflected the orange flames of the fire and she was dazzled, made blind, her hands still cold and her feet muddy, uncovered, carved from wood.

She let them stand her up beside Doctor Tscharner. She tolerated their absurdity. Their arms did not touch. He had no ring to put on her. He did not hold her hand. They stood and answered in their turn. She felt she was not there but was somewhere looking at it, looking at what was happening to her. She smelled the cold on him, the cold that came in with him from the black night, that crackled from his boots and hung in the sleeves of his cape. She watched and smelled and listened and made sounds with her mouth when they asked her.

Lentz went away alone, but Aaron Bloodworth stayed with them. He sat his demijohn in the middle of the floor, in the exact center of the braided rug, then examined Jonah's gun. She did not comprehend all that took place or in what length or amount of time it took to happen. She only understood the fire blazing and the black night banked up against the windowpanes.

Jonah and her pa rode up. Old Keith shouted, "Shanner, you got my gal?"

Aaron Bloodworth looked out and saw Jonah sitting on his horse. "Sassy as Satan," he reported, then called out, "Is that you, Jonah?"

Jonah grinned. He sang back, "Yeh, this's me. Straight from the Whale's gut!"

"Get your ass out of that door before I blast it off, Bloodworth!" bawled Keith. "That goddamned son-of-a-bitching German is who I want." He began pumping shots at the house.

Bloodworth slammed the door and fell to his knees. He was not hit, but he heard the splintering of glass and the crack of the gun, Jonah's gun, placed in Doctor Tscharner's hands by the girl.

The old man slumped against the neck of his horse. "God damn you, Shanner!" he screamed. "You liked to killed me! You crazy! Everybody knows you crazy! Cassie!" He straightened up and screamed louder than before. "Cassie, if you in there, you know he's crazy!" He whipped his horse over the cold stones of the Kelly Star Road and his son followed.

"They gone," said Bloodworth, peeping through the shattered window. A gust of sharp air struck his face and his eyes watered. He turned a marveling face to Doctor Tscharner, still standing with the gun aimed at the blackness. "You whupped 'em! You whupped their asses!"

Bloodworth stayed the night on Apion, draining the demijohn, marveling many times over. In the morning, he rode back home, his eyes red and the beard grown out over his chin. He told Hannah. She shook her head and lifted her skinny chin. "Ain't no good in that," she said, "ain't a bit of good."

18

Marriage had never occurred to them. They had neither wished for it nor avoided it. And they did not consider whether it was good or not, whether they were good themselves or not. They made their own world and walked about in it, walled off, kept apart, restricted. He continued to sleep in the surgery. He would not touch her. His mind placed her in seclusion. She became quiescent, like a pupa. She understood that it was not a punishment on her.

When the wedding was over, Doctor Tscharner had gone without a word to her. And she had accepted his arrangement willingly. She was like a root that had been taken out of the dirt, not jerked up carelessly, but dislodged by a steady willful fingering. And like the roots she prepared with her own hands, she began to scrape off her decay, her wilt.

She began by exploring her new tillage. The house had only four rooms on the ground level. She went through them noiselessly, cautiously opening the doors which he had shut. He had kept the slaves and the child from the parlor while they were being married by Lentz and while her pa and Jonah had cast their ugly noise against the house. Now she sought them.

The first bedroom she opened was the same size as the parlor and was wainscotted like it and had a high timbered fireplace with a mantel. In the adjoining room slept Lieschen. Her bed was railed on the sides and Pheny slept on the floor. Since the death of its mother, Pheny had not slept one night away from the child. There was no fireplace in this room and the china doorknob felt like a globe of ice in Cassandra's hand. She left the door open, thinking the warmth from the parlor fire would seep in and comfort the sleepers.

Behind the parlor and across the narrow hall from Lieschen was a dining room. It had a polished table with six polished chairs. A picture of harvest fruits hung on the wall. In the parlor, she had noticed two pictures. One was of flowers, done in wan colors like dust. The other showed two horses, their eyes bulging, their nostrils flaring, their hoofs flailing the thunderous air. And in the background was a jagged thread of lightning painted yellow against a blackish sky. Around each of these pictures was fastened a narrow black frame and the glass under which they were

147

pressed was wiped clean of fingerprints. Cassandra had never before seen pictures. She had never drawn pictures. And she wondered what made a person draw things. She did not connect drawing with lettering. Or with reading.

Tiny stairs led up to the loft rooms, two of them, each with a window of only four panes. These windows, cut into the wall quite close to the chimneys, were fastened against the wind by a wooden peg. In one of the rooms was a straw tick. She peered out of the dark loft window. She saw the fenced gardens, the sheds, the one with a wall of glass which glimmered feebly. There was no moon. And the only light came from the small stars, a thin greyish light, barely penetrating the air.

Cassandra shook her head. She lay down on the straw tick and fell asleep. In the morning, she woke chilled and with an unpleasant taste in her mouth. The bubble-streaked glass threw watery sunbeams on the floor. They wavered across her hand, distorting her bones and arteries, melting her nails like butter. She stood up feeling lost and unreal. She felt detached from her body the way she felt last night, detached, outside of herself. She had slept in her dress all night and it was wrinkled. The straw had left ridges on her cheek. She rubbed them. The sounds of breakfast reached her and she went down the tiny steps.

They sat at breakfast in the dining room and were served by the slaves. She did not know what to do with herself. Pheny scowled at her bare feet. The forks felt clumsy in her hands. Doctor Tscharner began to press apples in a small cider mill. He handed a tumbler over the table. The sweet smell of it rose in her brain and she began to vomit, convulsing with shame, her hands held over her face. He did not get up to help her.

Cassandra noticed, before she was carried from the room, that a grandfather clock stood in the southeast corner with a picture of the rising sun painted on its face.

So she slept in the loft rooms, where the roof sloped and she had to stoop to walk about. She liked it up there where no one had slept before her. She knew she could have the bed downstairs, but she did not want to lie in it until he did. She made up her mind that she could be no intruder in this house.

It grew colder. The wind stripped every leaf from every tree. They lay heaped on the ground and were covered by frost. They turned brown. The November rains pelted them and when the pallid sun came out the leaves did not glisten as in summer.

Cassandra pondered her new name. *Cassandra Tscharner*. She spelled it out and wrote it on a sheet of paper with ink. It sounded long. She enunciated it carefully, accenting the thick R's. She clenched her teeth and snarled the *Tscharner* so that it came out a plosive, abrupt, and with distinction. Her ear sharpened to the sounds of his speech and she began to imitate, to practice, and though her own speech remained as sparsely phrased as before, it took on a correctness, a pungence that had never been encouraged.

He did not restrict her. She wandered over Apion at will. The frozen earth spewed up in crusty red crystals. She dressed in the new clothing Pheny brought to her. It was well sewn, the seams smooth, straight, and the waists were made to loosen each month as she grew. She wore boots that fitted close as skin to her feet. They gave her a feeling of stature. She kicked the red frost and bent down stiff tufts of bracken with them. When she came back to the house, Pheny spoke to her. She knew that Pheny did not like her before, but Pheny had changed. She brought her a cloth dipped in alum water to wash her nipples. "You got to toughen," she said. And when she boiled salt meat, she saved a dish of the broth and gave it to Cassandra to use on the nipples. Often, as she sat in the kitchen where the fire crackled and the black pots gave off good smells, she would feel the child quickening and she wanted to bury her face in Pheny's lap, she wanted to be patted by Pheny, she wanted to be made to feel it was all right.

She did not approach Lieschen. The child sat and stared at her, sometimes wrinkling her forehead. Her eyes were full of black intelligence. She had a slate on which she made letters with a stick of chalk. They were clumsy letters, like broken white twigs. And she had a primer that spoke to her in sober little sentences. *A rude boy cries in the street. A red fox lurks in the wood. A round berry hangs from the thorn.*

Lieschen read them aloud, laboring with her finger pushed under each word until she reached the end of the sentence. And here she would announce triumphantly, "Period!"

Doctor Tscharner made his long journeys. They passed without any great reckoning. The days were shorter and shorter. It got dark earlier each week and the nights lengthened. He rode off with his cape wrapped close and

150

thick leggings tied on over his trousers. He went bare-headed, as usual, until the bitterness of the wind forced him to cover his ears.

Apion was cheerless. They went about their tasks like ants, scurrying through the cold to burn off the pastures, repair fence posts, dig compost pits. Ishmael padded the windows of the plant shed and put hot bricks from the fire around the plants to prevent their freezing during the long nights. Cassandra became tough, doing as Pheny had told her, rubbing the nipples with a piece of flannel when she went to bed at night. They became so hard she felt they were frozen and the pale colostrum oozed from the ends without her being aware of it.

Lieschen chanted the primer like a parrot. She drew on her boots with the chalk and Pheny scolded her. They sat stitching baby gowns, fashioning diapers with cloth tapes to tie at either side. Cassandra could not sew well. She stuck her fingers and bled on the gowns and that made Pheny irritable. She stopped trying to sew and began listing patients in the daybook while he was gone. It did not embarrass her that they looked at her big belly and pendulous breasts. She was immune to them. And when they had gone, she sat looking through the daybook. It interested her. She found others, old ones that went back for as much as five years. She found herself. It annoyed her that he could have phrased it so dispellingly: *Keith child, fracture, @ 1.50.*

Simultaneously, the same arm began to ache. She rubbed it. It was healed smooth and hard. Pale hair stood over the skin that had faded in its winter seclusion.

‡

The December nights were deadly cold. The first snow had fallen. She carried a fur rug to the loft with her and rolled in it. She was very large. The belly was a burden to her. She would be glad of her delivery. In the dining room below, the clock struck every hour clear as a church bell. Cassandra listened. She pictured the flames of the rising sun as it passed through the intervals marked for it. She dozed, a huge pregnant animal covered with fur.

Out in the snow, he could not tell the road from the riverbank. The whiteness confused him. No moon shone in the sky and he felt smothered by the dark. They crept home, like snails in the snow, the horse feeling for the blind road and the man feeling for the blind horse and a great black blindness weighing down the world around them. They started up the cheek of Apion Mountain. A tree limb knocked off his hat and his ears were filled with a rush of winter wind. Slowly, like snails, they crept until a faint low light showed ahead.

Cassandra pressed her cold hands to her pregnant belly and rejoiced in the warmth. The whir of the clock as it gathered together its coils and struck disturbed her. She heard a creak upon the stairs. She felt her body tense under the fur rug, lifting and prickling as though the fur were her own erectile tissue. She shut her eyes halfway, feigning sleep. A head rose on the stairs. He crawled over and put his face not two inches away from her own.

She did not want to open her eyes and look at him, but she couldn't help herself. His eyes were black as nightshade. And his thin patrician lips were serious. He let himself fall down beside her as he slipped an arm around her neck and kissed her on the lips.

"Cassandra." Her name glistened in his mouth like snow.

Doctor Tscharner was thirty-seven years old. He made his own world and its circumstances. He ignored the burden within Cassandra until it came forth in the dawn of a grey February morning. At first he thought there was no life to it. It came before its time and it would not cry. Then the cry it made filled every room of the house.

Down the steep ravines, a stroke of winter sunlight slit open the blackness. In the northern valleys, where rhododendron grew in the summer, the snow lay deep and unmelting. There it had snowed on top of snow on top of more snow.

Doctor Tscharner wrote in his log, repeating the words, the shapes of his circumstances, out loud.

February 27, 1833. Born this day a boy. I named him for my father, Cornelius Tscharner. Calm, fair. No wind. Extreme cold.

THE CYCLONE'
ten years later

19

She looked at him and thought, "I don't like you. I don't like you." There was no emotion in her. There was merely the thought. And his own emotion, as he looked back, was concealed. He saw much that disgusted him: a girl of fifteen, leggy, her hair loose on her back, her unrefined stare. He asked himself, "Who can she be?" Then his conscience answered him, "She is Lieschen." Her eyes stared black and hard like his own. Her hair, vibrantly yellow, beer-colored, was the last impression of Jeanne-Catherine Pons, the only visible trace of her existence.

"Do not come into the surgery when there are patients,"

he said. She went away without a reply. She tossed his words like she tossed her hair, not defiantly, but casually, a gesture of rearrangement. Her face was flushed. She was not a sullen child. She went gracefully.

"That your gal?" asked the blind man beside Doctor Tscharner.

"Yes," he replied. "It is Elisabeth."

"I could tell that was your gal," the blind man smiled and his eyelids rolled back. His blurred eyes did not reflect anything. The pupils were dim, indistinct. "I could tell by the way you tightened up. You was rubbing my finger joints and she come in. You tightened up on me really fierce." He sighed. "But you didn't hurt me no worse than I been hurt." He put his swollen fingers to his shoulder. "I got such wandering pains. It's the sudden change in the weather, I guess. I say it's up here and after a while it's down here." He clasped his knee. "Wandering pains. Gets worse at evening."

He stopped and sat looking mournfully around in his dark. He wore a large blue jacket that fitted him badly. Someone had pinned a pocket watch to his breast. It had a loop for a chain but there was no chain. He could not possibly read it in his blindness, but he frequently pulled the watch up to his ear and listened to its ticking as if to reassure himself of the passing of time. Every time he pulled the watch, a loose fold of the blue jacket came up with it. He spoke again, after listening to his watch's ticking. "My pa used to say old folks die off at the change of the weather. You'd hear tell of a lot of 'em dying in the first part of a hot spell, after a killing frost." His voice splintered. He fingered his watch and smoothed down his loose jacket. His eyeballs seemed to follow some moving thing across the opposite wall.

"Sometimes I see lightning, you know. Real bright and forked. Shooting through my eyes." He gestured with his hands, the blue cuffs of the jacket drooped over them. Doctor Tscharner gazed at him thoughtfully. He began to rub the joints with a piece of warmed flannel.

"Perhaps you only remember the lightning," he remarked.

"Oh, no, Doctor Shanner, I see lightning. In my mind's eye, I can *see* it shoot out and flash across!" He smiled again, rolling his eyeballs. "You's like my pa. My pa didn't never believe nothing but what he could see it for hisself." The blind man stopped and became silent, his eyes blinking, closing tight, then opening wide.

"I would suggest," said Doctor Tscharner, removing the flannel, "you immerse your body in a bath of warm salt water, strong with salt."

"I don't take to bathing," replied the blind man.

"Then pour warm water on your joints several times a day. On your fingers, your shoulders, your hips. Pour it out of a kettle straight from the fire. Pour it until you are soothed. A fomentation of mustard mixed with horseradish, maybe garlic, a little vinegar, as warm as you can bear, would help to ease you."

He took the blind man's arm and guided him to the door. A boy waited outside in a wagon. Doctor Tscharner took in the yard at a glance and saw Lieschen sitting in the plank swing on the porch. The boy and Lieschen were smiling. He scowled and looked away. The blind man beside him gave a soft chuckle and loosened Doctor Tscharner's fingers from his arm. "She must be around here again. My pa's a fool over his gals. I guess if you was to ast him what was the worst thing he could think of, he'd of said, 'A house full of gals!' "

He reached toward the wagon. The boy made awkward tugs at him as he swung himself over the side. He sat with his back to the boy and said, "He always said that, my pa did. And he always made out like he wanted boy children instead of girl children. But the truth of it was that it was the gals he favored." He punched the boy with his elbow. The boy flipped the reins and the mule plodded off. Doctor Tscharner leaned toward the blind man. "Avoid exposure," he warned, "of all kinds." The blind man nodded. He listened again to the ticking watch pinned on his breast, then drooped his head back against the plank that served as a seat for the boy. The boy hunched over the reins. There were ugly harness galls on the mule.

In the house, Lieschen took up a copybook and began to write out the conjugations for the French verbs she had learned. She turned the pages recklessly, tearing them occasionally, though not on purpose, and then began transposing the French into German. She touched the tip of her tongue to the steel quill, tasting ink. She put the quill back into the inkwell. She closed the copybook and rubbed at the ink on her fingers. Every thread of her skin showed in the places where the ink was absorbed. They looked like the undersides of leaves in autumn when they had turned dead and brown and split with their dryness.

It was nonsense, she thought. There was no one to whom

she could speak French. There were no Germans. In all her life, she had seen no Germans other than her father. She had barely seen enough people to know what they spoke beyond Apion Mountain. She spoke stiffly, when she spoke at all, mimicking Philip Tscharner. Cassandra Keith's dialect was a language all its own, containing sharp echoes of Doctor Tscharner superimposed on her native southern English.

Lieschen pieced together all the languages, the French in the copybooks, the German she heard from her father, the English she heard from him and from Cassandra, and the sounds that churned in the throats of the Negro slave people. She put it all together, declined, conjugated, but she rarely spoke it. She thought in it. She dreamed in it at night. But she refrained from its utterance. Speech, to her, was a terrible exposure, an uncovering.

Because she was a child and could not help herself, she taught her words to the only other child she knew, to Neil. He was a baby to her, but he used the words and made them more valid. He walked behind Pheny and he chattered the Babel sounds of Lieschen. The tiny bird-boned Negro stirred clothes in a washpot over a hissing fire. Then she hung them out and the small boy followed at her heels, cluttering the whole outdoors with his noises. Around and around the washpot, they trooped: Pheny with her steaming stick, poking the hot clothes, Neil with his relentless babble. Pheny grew annoyed. She turned on him and said, as if to dispel an evil influence, holding her stick, dripping, through the clouds of steam, "Shet yo mouf, chile." And he would shut his mouth.

161

For ten years, Lieschen had looked at all that passed. This house had its solar system. Things went through their appointed seasons, appeared at their times, flourished, gave forth, and were gone again. She suffered for nothing. Her benefactor, Doctor Tscharner, provided her with all comforts, except the pleasure of his company. He rode off on his black horse and returned two or three days later. He was occupied, distracted, asleep, engrossed, absent. The children grew and he was pleased. They were well; their teeth came forth; their brains developed; and their bodies took on the shapes of what they were. But for this joy, this pride in having progenerated herself and her brother, Lieschen could not discern in him the slightest sensation. He was like a cup of lukewarm tea faintly flavored with lemon rinds. And she had no taste for tea or for any beverage unless it was boiling hot or chilled with ice.

The Frenchwoman within whose body she had been nurtured and brought to perfection, the mother whose milk she had greedily sucked, the pale creature who doted on her, she could not recall. Sometimes, encountering certain scents, she was struck by a frustrating familiar feeling, the smell of roses full-blown and almost spoiled, dried lavender. But it was never anything she could point out. The cemetery in the woods she visited as a little girl with her father at vague moments. And she could not be entirely sure what it was that lay there. A slave's dog died and was buried in the woods. Mushrooms pushed through the earth with pine straws sticking to their white gills. She did not like the cemetery. The white obelisk, in her eyes, appeared ugly and out of place.

She watched her half-brother, Neil. He lay at first in a crib over which Pheny hovered like a small black bee. Later he crept on the floors, getting splinters in his knees. Pheny picked out the splinters and washed his knees. Neil became a special burden to Pheny. She held him all the time and would have prevented his learning how to walk. Her lap was forced upon him and he defecated in his diaper. He was angry and wanted to be free of her. He kicked his legs and pieces rolled out of his diaper. It smeared on Pheny's arms and a large piece fell into her apron pocket. The sight was unbearable to Lieschen. It was funny, revolting. She gagged as she smelled Neil; tears ran out of her eyes. She laughed and gagged. Cassandra shook her by the shoulders, then darted over and snatched Neil from Pheny. "No child of mine"—she screamed at Pheny—"no child of mine is going to wallow in his own shit! You hear me?" She screamed hatefully and pulled the diaper off Neil. She stripped him and washed him. Lieschen ran away, still gagging, choking. Her belly hurt from it. It was terrible. She could find no one to tie on to. There was not one of them that she could single out and proclaim.

And she did not truly want to. Doctor Tscharner was chiseled of steel. His edges would cut her hands. And this Cassandra, the mother of Neil, could exist on bare rock. She threw down roots and crushed the rock to sand. Doctor Tscharner's long absences, his rides, did not seem to disturb her. She knew where to find water when she was thirsty. She was not awed by steel or the smell of a baby's feces. Cassandra was a terrible creature. She slapped their hands, Neil's hands, Lieschen's hands, it did not matter to her whose hands. She slapped and said honestly, with no malice to distort her, "I wish you were both gone a hundred miles from here!"

Then in the night, as she lay alone, she could not bear what she had done to them. She rushed in to take Lieschen up, striking her with hard rough kisses that always hurt, blubbering foolishly to be forgiven. And Lieschen, half-asleep, starving for more blackness, complained and was glad when Cassandra had gone again.

She reached the age of fifteen. She recognized truth when she saw it. Often she would tell Neil as they played, she would look straight into his eyes, nailing him with the look, "I *know* the truth!" And Neil, the son, believed in her. He resembled his father, dark of hair, black eyes that were like his sister's, hard as volcanic glass, even to the long fingers of Doctor Tscharner. Pheny mused on it to Rutha. "He got the chirrum, all right. Nothing of either one of the mammy in 'em." And it was evident. His wives had been noncommittal in the unions that produced his son and daughter.

Doctor Philip Tscharner, chiseled of steel, with eyes flashing black like glass, his shoulders always straight, sat on his horse and commanded Apion Mountain. He lived up to his name among the natives. But he did not know the truth entirely. He had his daughter's way of looking straight at someone when he spoke. And it was unnerving and intense. He saw parts of the truth. He glimpsed it in dreams.

The sea came into his dreams, a pounding, thudding sea. And one wave of the sea dominated his dream. A monster wave reared higher than the ceiling, reared beyond the impossible boundaries of the sky, blue-greenish and black, with a flange of white on top. "This madness," thought Doctor Tscharner, sleeping with a terrible strength, drowning himself willfully. Grey-colored cold sand sank under his toes. The wave rushed.

He woke up. His throat pulsed madly and his skin was tight all over, prickling with little barbs. Cassandra slept, her skin smooth, tanned from exposure to the sun. Her breath smelled clean. The grandfather clock began to strike and the picture of the rising sun moved one flame.

20

As the little cylinder revolved, its warty protuberances picked at the ends of a long metal comb and they gave off tinkling vibrations. It was a waltz. There was nothing significant about it. The cylinder picked at the metal and the wooden box smelled oily. But other than the songs of birds and the human songs that came out of the mouths of Pheny and Rutha, this was the only music Lieschen had ever heard. Cassandra did not sing. She did not even whistle. Music played no part in her life. Lieschen, however, was absorbed by it.

She smiled approvingly at the music box and touched a

finger to the warts on the cylinder. They felt rough as a grater. She fitted the key and wound the box and listened and again smiled her approval. She did not like Neil to hear it. When he first entered her territory, she had pulled the music box from his reach and ran to the loft rooms and hid the thing far up under the eaves. Now she was older and more assured and merely closed the door to her room. She lay on her bed, listening, and quite often, for reasons she could not explain, the music box made her unhappy.

Clegg had a jew's-harp. He whanged at it. Whang, whang, whang, the sounds vibrated, bothersome, metallic, like the drone of monstrous bees. She asked to try it. She did not like to put the jew's-harp in her mouth after it had been in Clegg's, but her curiosity prevailed on her. She fitted it between her lips and struck it. The bent metal clanged against her teeth and pinched her lips. Its taste and feel were painful. Clegg grinned. "Looky here," he said, taking it from her. Whang, whang, whang. His black fingers strummed the peculiar little harp and his lips worked around it. Whang, whang. "Oh, stop," she said, and hurried away from the sounds.

The air was hot. The July grass was burned dry and yellow. The house lay shuttered against the afternoon and she was supposed to be inside, in her own room behind the closed door. She walked through the hot forest and her feet hurt in the boots. Her face was red. Her mouth itched, she fancied, from the taste of the jew's-harp. She came to the river, shining with a thick yellow skin clouded by mosquitoes. She parted the sassafras bushes and sat down to unlace the boots.

The water was unpleasantly warm, warm as blood, and

she curled up her toes, feeling the warm mud oozing between them. Lieschen wandered with no direction in the warm yellow river and a long time passed. She was not aware of the time. She all at once discovered herself standing still, listening for something. The river seeped around her and progressed heavily toward the sea. The river was unconcerned. Lieschen frowned and started to climb out. She was startled to find a young man standing in the trees looking at her.

She flushed darker with heat and surprise. She was not embarrassed. She felt very angry with herself for having been unguarded. She came out, pulling her dress from the briers growing on the bank. He continued to stare at her, his arms crossed over his chest, standing with his legs apart like a Colossus of Rhodes. His face had pale freckles. She put her hand to her own face, and when the fingers came down, they left white streaks across the red skin. He smiled. "I know who you are," he said.

They were repeating an unconscious pattern that had been set before them. The rhythm that had succored Cassandra Keith, the blindness that had immured Doctor Tscharner, came floating back in thin disguises. It had an uneasy innocence about it, making the pupils dilate abnormally, and producing profound sleep.

Lieschen did not care. She was like an underground root that sends up shoots to the surface from its top and at the same time sends down rootlets, deeper, from its lower part. That it was an unhealthy narcotic she was using to escape did not distress her. She only recognized her need. She had moldered too long on Apion Mountain. She felt she was coming awake after a long troubling sleep.

They did not have much to say to one another in the beginning. She knew who he was, too, from the one time she had seen him. It had been five years before, when she was ten and Neil was about two. Cassandra had taken them on a visit to her father's house. It was the only visit she had made to see him, and they went on a day when Doctor Tscharner was not there. They took a sack of vegetables and a jar of honey as presents. Clegg drove them there in the wagon.

It was an old house, big and full of drafts, with black spider webs swinging from the high ceilings. They went through it to the kitchen. There were lots of fireplaces like great black holes.

"That yonder my grandson?" asked the old man. Cassandra nodded. He picked up Neil and sat him in the middle of the kitchen table, turning him from side to side, peering at his ears, his eyes, even feeling the hair on his head. He stood back and announced in a voice that was partly prideful and partly disappointed, "I don't see nothing wrong with him!"

Cassandra took Neil and held him on her lap. "Yeh, Pa, you're glad, I suppose. I can see you are. It gives you something, doesn't it? Your girl, Doctor Tscharner's wife. Your grandson Neil."

"*Neil!* That ain't no decent name," he interrupted her. "Why don't you call him something decent?" He pouted in his chair, his head slumped, his horny wrinkled hands folded over his lap.

169

Cassandra waited for the pout to subside. Presently he peered up and his eyes fell on Lieschen. "That's hisn, ain't it?" he asked, grinning widely. "Her name's Lizzie. I heard tell of it." Lieschen moved behind Cassandra, her cheeks flushing dark, her ears prickling at every sound.

The old man tried to coax her to talk. He held out his hands and wiggled his fingers at her, wheedling, coaxing. She would not talk to him. Boone Keith entered the kitchen. He was a lean, hard-shaped boy, not as Cassandra had expected. Nothing was as she had expected. Jonah had given up looking for his vein of gold, had married, and now ferried the river. The old man sat in a chair by the kitchen fire. The veins in his hands were thick as roots. Jonah's wife was pregnant and her belly loomed high under her breasts. "I never expected to see any children of his," remarked Cassandra. She gave a dry glance to the wife.

The old man sighed. "Yeh, I know." He twisted in the chair. It was woven of cane and squeaked under him. Jonah's wife was not a glum person. She hummed and smiled at all of them, the strange glum Keith people. She did not question them, but drew two round cookies out of her apron. Neil took his eagerly and stuffed it in his mouth, grinning at her. Lieschen would not look at the woman. The woman talked kindly to her and slipped the cookie into Lieschen's stiff hand.

The old man tried to coax the child again, as if he wanted to make things right with her. At last he gave up and said, "That there is a *con*trary youngun." He rubbed his head. The hair in his nostrils had grown way out and quivered as he talked. "I know about *con*trary younguns. Every one of mine was borned *con*trary. Like bulls. They'd rip their guts out jumping over the fence to butt at me. No soppings in my crowd." He gazed longingly at the pregnant woman. "That's all gone now. Even Jonah. Even what he used to be is gone now. The marrow's been eat out of us."

Lieschen still stood rooted behind Cassandra, the cookie stiff in her fingers. The boy Boone made ready to leave. "Boone," said Cassandra, "take the children out with you."

He hesitated, surveying her and the two children, his old father, the pregnant wife of his brother. He nodded pleasantly. "Go on," said Cassandra, pushing at Lieschen.

Neil followed. There was a raccoon in a cage that stood on legs. "See," said the boy. The raccoon held up his little paws. They were like hands, black and tight, the skin as smooth as a pair of black gloves. Neil rattled a stick against the cage. The animal bared his teeth and made a churlish growl. "No," said Boone. "What you want to fret him for? Leave him be. He likes to live as much as you."

He turned away with disgust and refused to talk. They stood and looked at the raccoon and he wandered angrily in his cage, looking back at them, growling, the hair raising up from his neck. It was a frustrating and pitiful situation. The two children could not be rescued by themselves. At last the boy spoke. "Coons are curious. If you stand a mirror up against a tree, a coon will stay there and look at it all day, waiting for the other coon to do something." He smiled at Neil.

Lieschen moved back from the cage. She did not like the raccoon. He repelled her with his thick ringed tail, the black mask around his eyes. And it disappointed her that his growl sounded like the growls of dogs. She threw her cookie to the chickens in the yard. She noticed the ferry halfway across the river. She could hear the passengers talking to the ferryman.

She went back to the kitchen and took up her place behind Cassandra. And when they had returned to Apion and Clegg had put up the wagon, she forgot about the raccoon in the cage and about the boy. Cassandra never took them there again. The old man died in his bed. Jonah's wife was delivered of a healthy child and became pregnant again with another. The ferry went across the river and came back each day. Doctor Tscharner went across the river and returned. Lieschen filled her bones with rich marrow. She was young. Boone was young. The terrible power of their youth was a burden to them. The narcotic was strong and deadly, soothing, dilating. They disappeared into the trees. "Help me to get away," she said. "Help me," he echoed. "I'll show you something you ain't never seen in your whole life!"

The water was low and long shelves of rock jutted out from the river bed. The water eddied around them and the watermark could be plainly seen. It stood out as a long stain of brown, stretching for miles down each side. The foliage that grew above it was dingy.

Lieschen followed him. He led through the woods to a place below the mouth of the Uwharrie River, where the Council flowed off from it. "Looky," he said.

She cupped her hands. The remains of a stone ford rose above the low water. Parts of it were broken, but the greater mass of it lay in a pattern of sharp angles, zigzagging across the river. "Come on." He took her to the edge and, holding her hand, began to step out. The river offered

172

them no challenge. The rock was hot and dry. The brown algae growing over it had shriveled. It felt scratchy under Lieschen's feet. A thick fetid odor hung over the water.

They reached the middle and he stopped. "They were smart," he said. Lieschen gazed at the yellow water slipping around the rock. "They built this going back'rds and for'rds. You know why they done it like this?" She shook her head. "Going back'rds and for'rds separates the water. It ain't so forceful that way. They were sure smart."

"I don't know who you are referring to." Lieschen scratched at the algae with her toenails. It came away in little brown shreds and sprinkled on the water's surface.

He smiled at her prissy detachment. "Of course you don't. They were all dead and gone before you were ever thought up. Cherokee. Cherokee Indians." He motioned her back toward Larkin. "You seen how it is. We won't go further. I have been all the way. There's a hole near the middle, as big as a man. You have to jump there." He gazed at the long angled stone. "You got to confess it was smart."

They went back. The pebbled bottom had been uncovered by the shrink of the river. Boone began poking around. Some stones he picked up and some he cast away, skimming them across the yellow slick water. Lieschen climbed the bank and sat down in some shade. She watched him. The back of him was dark with sweat. The hair grew in kinks over his sunburned neck and the skin of his face never failed to impress her with its smoothness. She envied it. It was finer than her own, though tanned and freckled. It made her look sallow. "A waste," she thought, and wrinkled her nose.

He dropped a handful of pebbles; they clattered on the

hard dry beach, then he climbed beside her. "I found a big pot once washed up." He sketched in the air a large urnlike shape. "It looked like a big old gourd, the color of brass. But it wasn't brass. I kept it for a long time, then one of Jonah's brats busted it."

He lay back with his arms behind his head. There were dark circles on the armpits of his shirt. Lieschen smelled the sweat from him. And also the smell of the drying river algae. And the thick hot smell of woods, a smell of pitch and resin. She did not move. Trumpet creepers trailed from the branches. They made her itch to look at them. Their orange-scarlet funnels stretched open, aggressively luring the insects, though silent and without much perfume.

"Talk, Lizzie. Why don't you ever talk? Say something."

"I say enough."

"Yeh." He gazed up through the pine frond. "Yeh, you talk aplenty."

She turned sharply. He slanted his eyes and smiled. "You not wearing your shoes again," he remarked, eying her feet. "Someday you'll go to put 'em on and you'll find your foot's spread."

It made her angry for him to chide her. She clenched her teeth. "I don't care. I'm tired of being laced up."

"I don't see that you been laced up. All you got to do is eat and sleep." He continued to stare upward, smiling. A lump of yellow mud was balled under his toes. She hated it. She hated his words, which settled on her like spots of sunlight fretting black water. "You never had to work, Lizzie."

She fled from the sound of him, hating him unreasonably, scrubbing the sound out of her ears. At last she sank on the ground beside a great oak tree. Ants ran up and down in the bark, intent, wasting no movements. She gazed at them for some time, then balled her fist and smashed them individually, one after one after one.

She returned to Apion, her feet laced in the boots, the bonnet tied. She carried a handful of brierberries in her pocket. She did not expect to find Doctor Tscharner. He had come back sooner than was customary.

"Where have you been?" he asked, not unkindly, absorbing all of her appearance.

She was confronted with the possibility of lying. It presented itself to her and she found it appealing. But she chose to reject it. She pulled the berries from her pocket. "See, I was only looking for these." She held them out, innocent and plumpish, black as her own eyes. They rolled in her palm. One was bruised and left a violet stain. "I was only looking." Her toes bulged uncomfortably inside the boots. She was hot. The smell of the river wafted from her. Healthy bumblebees buzzed in the catalpa trees that grew in a row behind the kitchen. Pheny clanged supper pots.

Doctor Tscharner held the saddlebags in his hand. The leather was dusty and cracked. It reminded her of the algae on the Indian ford. "Yes." He took a berry and tasted it. "They are ready." He said this and left her, the brown dry saddlebags flapping against his leg.

He knew she was lying. He did not know how she could do it, but he saw the marks clearly on her. It came back to him in a single piercing instant. The pungence was unmistakable and he regretted it sorely. He thought of what he should do. The humiliating memory of old Keith flared through him, its sounds, its October shadows, the severe insuperable honor, the vulgar haste.

He would not do that. Lock up Lieschen in the loft. Load his gun and tamp down its wadding to insure the shot. Fire at the first man or boy, gentleman, lout, who might come to take Elisabeth Tscharner from this place. The rarity of her blood could not be robbed like that. He would continue to trust her. He could not permit suspicion to blemish his practice. He could not heal by subterfuge.

21

"Look at him!" Neil pointed rudely at A. D. "Look at all that!"

A. D. sat on the kitchen logs calmly lacing up his shoes. He had on two pairs of thick woolen stockings and had rolled his pants legs down below his ankles. The shoes were heavy-soled, as cumbersome as stumps. "I ain't getting bit by no snake," replied A. D. "I ain't going swell up and die." He jerked at the leather strings. A. D. was no longer a child. He stood as tall as Ishmael, but was built with bones as light as Pheny's. When he had finished lacing his shoes, he took the pails and led Neil and Lieschen to the patch of brierberries. It was still early and a heavy dew lay on the ground. The clear small drops sparkled. Lieschen felt pure as the wet dew. She felt she could exude small drops and cling to each blade of grass.

They came into a meadow where the sun had split open the air and was shining in white layers. Lieschen's feeling went away. The brierberries grew in a dense thicket around the edge of the meadow. They were frustrating. The brambles pierced and were hard to separate. The berries flourished in several generations simultaneously. A. D. professed to be able to distinguish them: red were last year's, green were next year's, and the deep purple belonged to this year's yield. They began filling the pails. The white fingers turned violet and reddish. A. D.'s black fingers looked wetter and blacker. He stripped the berries quickly. They fell into his pail making a hollow drumlike sound.

Lieschen began to eat hers. They tasted warm. She rolled them between her fingers. They were round and dark and shiny as the eyeballs of mice. She stopped picking and crossed to the edge of the meadow where everything was still cool and dewy. She sat down and pulled out the laces of her boots. When her feet were free, she rubbed them through the dew. Gooseflesh crept over her.

A. D. looked disapprovingly at her naked feet. "You better not step in that dew. Dew ain't healthy. If you got a sore, that dew'll fester it."

"I don't believe it," she murmured. She put the boots in the fork of a limb and amused herself by walking through the dew as long as it lasted. And when it was evaporated, she walked in the meadow and around the pine trees, rubbing her feet over the rough cones. Neil and A. D. picked their pails full. The sky was white with sunlight and the meadow shimmered with its heat. Neil spotted a full cluster of berries high over the middle of the brambles. He reached for it, going up on tiptoe, unconsciously thrusting one foot deep in the wild grass beneath.

Unexpectedly, he began to scream. And his scream surpassed any that he had ever uttered in his life. Lieschen's heart palpitated and she scrambled to where he had fallen backward on the grass, jerking his foot violently. "I been bit! I been bit! I know I been bit!" His piercing repetitions stunned both his sister and the Negro. A. D. picked up the foot. The punctures were evident, small, evenly spaced, as though two needles had been driven in his flesh. Two dots of blood appeared on his skin. Neil stopped screaming and began to cry, unabashedly, before them.

"That viper still in yonder," said A. D. grimly. "You help him back, Miss Lizzie. I ain't going leave till I kill that viper." He crept toward the brambles cautiously and reconnoitered them with his huge frightened eyes. Lieschen put Neil's arm around her neck and helped him hobble away. She hesitated when she had crossed the meadow and looked back at A. D. He was taking a big rock from the pile that lay at the side of the meadow. He weighed it in his hand, then cast it down, and selected another.

"My foot feels like it's frozen," said Neil, sobbing and wiping his face on his sleeve.

"Come on, hurry." She pulled him through the woods. Doctor Tscharner was still at home when they got to Apion. She stopped and shouted at Ishmael to come and carry Neil. Ishmael took him from her and carried him to the surgery. Pheny hurried after them, clucking and scold-

179

ing. Cassandra followed behind Pheny, looking perplexed, worried, vaguely annoyed at all the fuss Neil was causing. Doctor Tscharner proceeded rapidly with his examination. Lieschen surveyed all of them. They moved like symbols in a miracle play.

Neil had been bitten on the ankle and it had swollen so big his boot had to be cut off. The leather split like an old skin. Doctor Tscharner took hold of the wound. It was so perfectly punctured that it somehow angered him. He bound a tight ligature above it and etched a line from one puncture to the other with his lancet. The line turned red. The tiny red punctures lost their identity in it. "Bring sweet oil," he said. He rinsed his mouth and, being careful not to swallow, he began to suck the wound.

When this was finished, he ordered a cataclysm of quick-lime and brown soap and smeared it over the injury. He took down a demijohn of Bloodworth's corn liquor, which he always kept on hand. Cassandra crushed red pepper pods and Doctor Tscharner stirred in the liquor. They gave it to Neil. The boy choked and threw back. Doctor Tscharner forced it in. The sweetish smell of the liquor spread through the surgery. Neil whined. He rolled his head on the pallet and the straw inside it crackled like dry leaves.

All of them had something to do, some part to play. Doctor Tscharner had met the need of his stricken son. He got up to wash the smells off his hands and he noticed his daughter's feet. She stood round-eyed between Cassandra and Pheny. Her feet were wet, naked, and white as mushrooms. Pine straws stuck between her toes.

A. D. brought back the boots. They lay on top of the berry

pails. She took them from the kitchen. He had brought the snake, too, stretched over a stick, its head mangled to a coppery mush. It measured four feet, and when they laid it in the dust, the limber body continued to weave; the nerves and muscles could not forget easily. The tip of its tail was like a delicately pointed copper needle.

"Don't you dast leave that snake around here!" screeched Rutha from the kitchen.

"He daid. He ain't going nowhere," replied A. D.

"I don't care. He got a mate! She ain't daid yet."

A. D. took the snake away, the tail still curling, and buried it. It was now late afternoon. Neil lay drugged on the peppered liquor. His foot had swollen until no division was visible between the ankle and the rest. The venom was deterred. Doctor Tscharner felt certain of it. The boy did not appear delirious. He did not complain of pains. He only wanted to sleeep undisturbed. Cassandra pressed juice from boneset. The bruised leaves lay wilting in a saucer. Night came on like a hot dark curtain.

Lieschen went to bed. It was so sultry she could not draw a breath in ease. Doctor Tscharner, his wife, and Pheny remained with the boy. Neil slept, oblivious of the heat and the insects falling around the lamps, and his breathing sounded correct. Doctor Tscharner opened the log and began to write. Cassandra listened to the scratching of the pen, the clumsy bumping of the insects, and the regular inhale and exhale of Neil. Pheny dozed. The skin of her eyelids was thin and black and the veins in it twitched. After a long silence, Cassandra said, "What are you writing?" And then she added, "Philip?"

He stopped. He did not answer her immediately. He

looked at her with his long directness. When he blinked, it was almost imperceptible, and his black eyes were not marred by it. "Of this day," he replied. He dropped his eyes to the page and continued.

"Of this day," she thought, "of this day and of all the days long past and to come to be." It comforted her. Then it made her uneasy. A terrible cosmic force took hold of her and she felt the intensity of all those past and future days. A tiny disc of light beamed at the end of it, like light leaking through the cracks of a black cellar hole. There was a sick, despairing feeling about it, one that would make a butterfly beat his wings to threads trying to get away.

"He stirring," whispered Pheny hoarsely. She had wakened and crept to the pallet. Neil opened his eyes and looked at her fondly. He began to smile. His eyes glittered black as stars and the light from the lamps made his face yellow. Doctor Tscharner studied him, feeling his pulse. Cassandra lifted a spoonful of boneset to his mouth, but he would not accept it. He stubbornly smiled, his teeth clenched, the yellow light reflecting in his eyeballs. She poured it into his mouth. It ran out both corners in a thin green trickle.

"I don't like that look in his eye," murmured Cassandra. "It reminds me of when my ma died." She stood up and set the saucer on the table. The spoon dripped on her apron. "She died in the night, like this, a warm night. I was in the room. She died, but her eyes kept on staring at me, following me around, looking. She had given up the ghost, but her eyeballs hadn't." She looked at Doctor Tscharner. Her voice wavered. "He's got the same look."

"Nonsense." Doctor Tscharner took his lancet. "I am going to open the wound," he said, moving a lamp to the floor beside Neil. The boy suddenly jerked. Still smiling, he looked around at all of them, his burning eyes resting briefly on each one. Then he smiled moronically at his grim and sensible father, poised with the grim and sensible steel, and he said clearly, with no fuzziness of tongue, "Don't mess with me, Papa."

In the house, Lieschen dreamed. She was not asleep. It was too hot. She lay in the bed and squeezed her eyes shut. If she concentrated, she could take herself backward through the numbers beyond *three*, *two*, *one*, *zero*, into infinity. When this happened, she fancied the walls and ceiling burst asunder and she was projected into an unlimited blackness spangled with white flakes of light. It seemed, though she could not be sure, that the blackness had a curvature to it, along the northeastern expanse, and that a narrow ridge of reddish light burned just above this curvature.

She squeezed her eyes harder and gritted her teeth. It was a temptation not to open up and dissolve the whole mirage. She concentrated harder. The beetles began screeching in the woods. She was conscious of the animal rustlings, the twittering of the fowl, small anxious sounds, heartbeats, the condensing of the dew. She scrunched down in her bed, drawing up her knees like a fetus. The blackness became a womb. The moon beamed, huge and yellow, a febrile egg, pulsating in tiny red veins. She ran backward through the expended day, through the yards and fields of the morning, through the forests of the afternoon and into the plateau of the night. And in this night, the moon and stars issued out of its black uterus and the firmament gave up its ghost. The

183

lesser lights and the revolving spheres appeared to be falling, colliding, dissolving away into showers of fire.

A long green river coiled below her. She swung herself into the bottom branches of a giant oak tree. Slipping, scratching her face on the warty bark, eroding the skin on her palms, she climbed. The sweat trickled down her back and she smelled the sweat. She relished the smell of it. She climbed on persistently through the dark body of the tree. Balls of fox fire glowed over the green river, smelling of decay and rancid oil. She drew up all the smells, breathing hard, scratching at the bark of the tree with vigor.

Doctor Tscharner came to the bank of the river and called her name. "Elisabeth Tscharner." She climbed on. Up and up, ever up, parting the limbs, stabbing her feet into the pits of limbs, tearing away leaves and twigs, hard green bunches of the acorns. She did not cease until she clung, breathless, to the top. Below her spread the dark earth, encircled and honeycombed by the green river. To the north, the east, the west and south departed the horizons of the planet. And she clung here, to this green navel string that had not ulcerated or become separated from her, and inside her burst a terrible thing. She was wearied from the rupture.

"Elisabeth Tscharner," he called again, and his voice rang over the darkness like a blade of steel, sharpened with deadly sin. He got down from the black horse and put his hand on the tree. She let go with both hands. She fell.

22

There was an illness in Weymouth across the river. Doctor Tscharner prepared his saddlebags and rode off. His son had resisted the poisonous bite of the copper-colored snake and healed under a straight pinkish scar. "I don't feel anything in it," said Neil, running his fingers across the band of tissues. "It's like a dead place. I think I feel some nerves around the edge, but I'm not sure I do."

"It's all right," said Cassandra. "He fixed it right. Don't scratch at it."

Doctor Tscharner crossed the ferry. Jonah Keith was no longer his tormentor. They ignored one another. There were fish breaking the water everywhere. Their agile bodies glistened and the splash of the water was distinct in the air. One broke so close to the ferry, Doctor Tscharner saw its gills fan outward to embrace the air. The water had begun to rise a little and regain its swift current.

Jonah was curious about the saddlebags. "You going over for long?"

Doctor Tscharner was not fraternizing. He replied, "There is a spreading malignancy in Weymouth County. I shall be over more than two days."

Jonah set him ashore. There were two wagons waiting. They drove aboard and he began the backward passage. He asked them of the malignancy and they affirmed it. Jonah shook his head. "Why don't he never come down with it? With *nothing?*" He gestured at Weymouth, at the road where Doctor Tscharner had vanished. He looked at his passengers and marveled, "I ain't never heard tell of him being sick." They all soberly agreed.

"I have come to see Miss Lizzie; you know it." He smiled at his sister. He bent down and wiped the dust from his boots.

"Boone." Cassandra was puzzled by him. She perceived a stranger in this appearance of the relic-child from her past, Boone, the castaway. She did not want him to be here, yet she could not dispel him. "Boone," she repeated firmly, "What do you want to see her for?"

Lieschen came to the door behind her. She flickered a brief smile when she saw it was Boone, but she was not overjoyed. His quiet and persistent good humor amused her. "Come in," she said, stepping around Cassandra.

"I am," he replied, and advanced up the stoop.

Cassandra drew in her breath. "Wait," she murmured, glancing rapidly at both, catching the blurred smile on Lieschen, translating the gentle rebellion in Boone. "Wait right there."

Boone stopped. "You don't need to fly up, Cassie." His tones were slow and well oiled. "Besides, I know what's fretting you. And I saw him cross the ferry with Jonah yesterday. He's not coming back this evening. No need for you to fly up." He smiled at her so positively that she felt blinded by it.

"You came here because of that?" Lieschen let a kind of sneering slide over her voice. She narrowed her eyes. Boone was delighted with the challenge. He parried, "I came here because of a lot of things, the least of which was Doctor Shanner."

"It does not matter." Cassandra looked down the road. She habitually looked down the road whenever his name, his thought, came into her mind. "Listen to me. This just can't be." She flushed. She noticed Lieschen smiling openly this time, her black eyes flashing. Again she felt blinded and it made her angry. "Well, what are you laughing at?" she snapped.

"Nothing," replied the girl, and closed her mouth primly. Boone ran a hand over the back of his head. The hair was wet and shiny. "Well, are you all going to invite me to sit?"

"No, no, you can't sit down. Not now." Cassandra implored them both and she hated herself for doing it. "Lieschen," she said, "tell him."

Lieschen remained silent, arrogant, walled off. She pinched the columbine that grew around the porch railing.

"Boone?" Cassandra saw it was no use. "I could strangle

both of you. I could grind you into mincemeat. I could stomp you into the ground until you were nothing but two greasy places!" She threw up her hands. "All right, all right. I see this is the way it is. But it is not my fault." She went inside the house.

Lieschen pinched the columbine again. A dark bruised place spread over the thin little stems. She leaned over the railing and her yellow hair fell, covering her face from him. She drummed her fingers on the railing. "Why did you come here?"

"To see Miss Lizzie," he replied, "and what difference does it make?"

"You did not. And it makes a lot of difference." She squeezed the railing, but she did not raise her voice to scream at him the way she would have liked. "You came for a spite to him. I *know* the truth." Lieschen turned furiously and fixed him with a hard black gaze. He took hold of Lieschen and kissed her with a terrible mastery. Lieschen would not relinquish her gaze. She examined him minutely. His eyebrows grew in a straight line. The freckles were light-colored, like dots of dust across his face. His nostrils flared out, then back in. He released her.

"I don't know much," he said quietly, "but dirt farming. And you hate dirt farming. You told me so yourself. But I know what I am. And that's a lot more of knowing the truth than what you fancy yourself." He smiled again and his smile was uncomfortably positive. "Your lips feel hot, Lizzie."

Rage rolled in her and she fought for some cruel thing to throw out at him. But he had retreated. He took the stoop at one leap and strode down the slope. She stood by the railing and watched him go. The bruised frail columbine wilted. Her pointed fingers drummed the smooth grey rail.

The summer dryness passed. The river recovered and the ferry made its trips. Doctor Tscharner rode as always, brought new lives into the light, took diseased and injured and exhausted lives out of it. He often felt a great morbidness in him. It came like a foul-smelling vapor that he was forced to inhale. And then it was cleared away. His children on Apion suffered morbidity, too, but theirs was not cleared away. It was too sanguine and too deeply colored red.

Neil could remember little of the night when he lay in the surgery, smiling like an idiot. Something had begun to change within him and he projected it onto the world. The girl who was his sister, half his sister, had changed, too, had become something different to him.

They studied as before, sitting at the polished table in the dining room. But it was changed. He felt a homesickness mixed up with the geography. He read about harbors, imports, exports, prime meridian, the tundra of Russia. Lieschen had a compass with which she inscribed arcs and perfect circles, bisected, angled, erected, twisting it agilely from her wrist. She raised the faces of geometry all over her paper. And when she had finished with geometry, she pursued algebra. Theorems, formulae, all of it passed before her solved and resolved, equated, canceled. It irritated him terribly and made him jealous, the way she coped with numbers, the way she took hold of the intangible and shaped it, proved it, solved it.

And his feelings persisted. His homesickness for her, his irritation and his jealousy were like a faint lingering of sweetness that had become stale. They floated up from dark places, empty places, and brushed by his face. He stood blinking in the half-opened doors. This was the dying, the autumnal, yellowed hazy feeling of Lieschen, who had gone and left him behind; who had left him her ghost, yellow and wan and smelling of dead fireplaces. And after he had stood blinking, his cheeks glowing like coals in the awful gloom, he closed the doors. She was gone.

And the person who had come in her old place forced him to a terrible knowledge. She showed the truth. And he was bitterly grateful. The truth had always been there in some form. It was in the affectionate terror he had at first felt for his mother, Cassandra, in the warm pulsing of his infant's body. He grew older, his soft body grew harder, and he exchanged the cosy terror for a comfortable indifference. Cassandra was never maternal. She did not nurture with her voice or her womb. Her breast was tough, the nipples never cracked or bled from the sucking. And she felt no tender delight in nursing him and was relieved to wean him. But it was wrong to think her unkind. She was exceedingly kind. She wanted people to be comfortable, to be healthy and warm and fed. She damaged no thing. But what mattered most to her was Doctor Tscharner. This was the centrifugal force in her life, the thing that took hold of her and whirled her around and separated her from all other impediments.

If a great plague had come out of the sky and carried off her son and the daughter that belonged to her husband, she would have sorely grieved. But within the month, through the incessant washing of days and nights, the hurt would have healed of its own accord.

Neil recognized this and he did not resent it. It would be the same should Cassandra be stricken down. Nothing would waste among them. Their mutual symbiosis had ended with the division of the umbilicus.

But for Lieschen he now felt a terrible waste. A door had been shut and it worried him that he had not stopped it in time, wedged it open, or destroyed it utterly. When he was little, he had been made to lie down in the early afternoon and take his rest. The windows would be opened and the careless noise of the birds drifted through. They would lie together, Lieschen's long yellow hair streaking the pillows, beads of moisture on her face. She whispered in spasms to him.

"And then the bears came out of the woods and they ate up the little children and their claws scratched like this!"

The rasp of her nails shuddered down into his uneasy stomach. He trembled and looked at the little furrows they had made on the sheet.

"They scratched and they scratched, like this, and when they had eaten up all the little children, devoured every hair and bone, they yawned and rubbed their bellies and went back to the woods and lay down and slept contentedly."

He would shut his eyes tightly against the annoying sunlight and his ears would quiver. He lay so still she thought he was asleep and got up and left.

Now it could not happen. If he fell asleep, it first was memorized in trickling and creaking, blood, sinews, sweat. Lieschen was bad to have told him such a tale when he was little. He found he could get very angry at Lieschen and he indulged himself.

It became unbearable. He fled the house where she was.

191

Horse nettles flourished on the road, flowering white, with yellow berries. They reminded him of his sister. And the straw-colored barbs stung. He tramped over the mountain, and when he came home, Boone Keith sat on the porch with Lieschen and kissed her.

He spied on them. He followed Lieschen if she left. He faded from tree to tree behind her and his eyes absorbed all her guilt. In the night, he dreamed such ferocious dreams. He put his hands on Lieschen. She beat him and pushed him. Her naked breasts dazzled him. The nipples were hard as acorns. He ran away from her. He looked in the mirror and saw his face being covered by millions of white freckles. He felt tumescent. He wanted them punished. Their recklessness chafed him. And his bad dreams humiliated him.

It did not take many days. He met his father on the Kelly Star Road and he told him of Lieschen and Boone Keith. When it was told, he was ashamed. He held on to the bridle of the horse and blubbered like a fool. "Don't tell Lieschen it was me," he begged, "please don't." Doctor Tscharner was displeased. "Go away," he said.

He rode to Apion and went into the house. Lieschen sat on the tiny staircase. She was idle, her hands empty. That made things worse. He began speaking to her intently, his voice straining against the tumult of his displeasure. "I have kept you in my house. I have taken care of you well. Elisabeth!" His black cape limped around his knees, the hem was powdered with the dust of his journeys.

"Taken care of me?" Lieschen sat stubbornly on the stairs. She knew the source of his displeasure, but she refused to recognize it. She was a warrior maiden with glittering black spears and breastplates of silver. She laughed carelessly. "How aesthetic you are."

Cassandra stood watching them, the girl on the stairs and the tall black-caped man before her. Neil crept through the door. Lieschen saw his tears. She knew it was Neil who had betrayed her and so she cut him off. He heard the knife whistle through him. And then he was castrated a second time. For he had betrayed not only his sister, but also his mother, Cassandra. She who scratched at insect bites on her legs and smelled sometimes of sweat, she who helped slit open the pig at slaughter, possessed a deity of her own. And now she was defiled, betrayed. He had done it to them. He hung his head when she said fiercely to him, "Cornelius, leave us."

The shame of it entangled him like a spider web, delicate and virulent, heartless, radiant with dewdrops. He walked away and slammed the door hard to convince them. Then he pressed his eardrum to near bursting against the wood. The sounds came, strained, but distinct and poisonous.

She was sent away to school in the city of Raleigh. The crops and flowers, vines and trees faded in season, shriveled, dripped in the rain. Her teachers sent reports of her progress, which was always excellent. She did not write letters to them. Neil's curiosity clung in his brain. His shame would not rest. "She knows the truth," he told himself. But it did not absolve him. Lieschen's guilt had ceased to exist and there was only his. And he returned, more than once, to those empty places, those half-opened doors, and stood motionless, as old people will stand in front of a fireplace, rubbing their hands, whether there is a fire burning or not.

23

Winter came hard. People marveled at the severe winds. From the first frost into the first snow, the long months pulled themselves laboriously and the wind bit into the people with edges of steel. The world was at a solstice. Sometime late after the passing of the winter constellations, snow lay on the ground fifteen inches deep. It piled up in the ravines and hung on the boughs of the pines, bending them over with its great weight. The sun came out and shone briefly each day, not enough to cast any shadow, then departed behind the mist. And underneath the snow lay solid ice. The river froze. Out in midstream the channel ran under a thin yellow pane. At places it broke through the pane and bubbled up, then sank again.

A heavy white settled over the Kelly Star until there could be seen no distinction between road and forest. It crept up the slope to Doctor Tscharner's house and weighted his roof under thick blankets. The frozen firs looked like spumes of sea water. The obelisk stuck up from a drift of whirling white.

At Bloodworth's mill, the overshot wheel was frozen. Pieces of ice, shards and lumps, piles of broken icicles, like broken teeth, lay over the crust of the snow that covered the dam. The windows were loaded with snow. He had shoveled a path up the hill to his house.

Hannah Bloodworth, the wife of Aaron, made hominy. She selected the ears with the finest grain and shelled them into a black kettle. They boiled over the fire for two days and nights. She put fresh wood to the fire. "Don't you dast spit in my ashes," she warned her husband. He grumbled in reply and dozed.

When she was satisfied the time was right, Hannah took up a shovelful of the cleanest, whitest ashes and dashed them into the kettle. The lye eroded the tough husks from the kernels, laying them bare and white, with a generous sprinkling of yellow. Hannah stirred. The steam reddened her face. She took a knife and, wrapping herself warmly in her blue shawl, with three pairs of woolen stockings on her feet, she struggled through the snow to the smokehouse. She cut a long slice of ham from the carcass hanging on a hook. The heavy rind of salt and pepper crumbled in her fingers. The rancid odor filled her nose. She took it back and cut it into strips and washed it. Then she laid it in her skillet and sat the skillet on a tripod over the flames. The fat curled and turned crisp. The hominy thickened. "Smells good." Aaron stretched and stood up, his knees creaking.

They fell to eating. It was a long winter and they had been imprisoned in the house for months. The dim, gloomy days and blind, black nights had drained them of their usual interests. They were like familiar strangers to each other. "This snow'll lay a lot of folks up for a while," observed Bloodworth, peering out the windows on either side of the fireplace. A small carved clock ticked on the mantel. Its grey-colored pendulum swung in short arcs, not much more than the space of an eyeblink.

"Yeh," she responded. She unpinned her shawl and drew it up closer. "Days like this, James would set his traps for birds."

Bloodworth spat into the ashes. "I remember them traps," he muttered. "You think a smart of James. But he won't nothing. There was something wrong with that youngun. I always knowed it. You never knowed it." He turned toward her, hoping for a retort. Her chin quivered, but she remained silent. The hominy continued to bubble in the kettle. She scraped the bottom with her spoon. The white porridge stuck to it. She rapped it on the rim. "Them traps was bad, I admit. But he didn't truly bother nobody with 'em." She moved before the windows. "I can see him out yonder in the cleared place. He'd set them traps and put crumbs all around to bait the birds."

Bloodworth stamped his feet under the table. The dishes clattered. "And then he'd come trucking back in with them birds all skint and dressed and stick 'em over the fire and roast 'em. God! I can smell them stinking things yet! Then he'd sit down over there with a cold bistit and eat 'em, black and nasty and half-raw." He hurled the words at her. "What do you suppose he was eating, woman? Robins? Blue jays? Sparrows?"

"Oh, Aaron!" She jerked her shoulders irritably and her voice became stronger. "You know there ain't no robins around here in the winter!"

Aaron Bloodworth let his head fall against the back of his chair, shutting his eyes like a martyr. "God," he said, as if to exclaim to the world his utter desperation.

The thick dishes sat on the table growing cold, greasy with pork gravy. Hannah smiled. James did not like pork. It had not seemed right that a Larkin County youngun wouldn't like pork. But then there had been many things James had not liked. She gazed out the window. It was turning darker, the shadows under the pines looked blue, the sky grey as pigeons. *Maybe pigeons, he ate?* She glanced at Aaron. He was sulking about James. The merest mention of James this long winter passage would conjure up whirling dervishes of bitterness. She moved to the table and the boards creaked in the floor. "I'm going to wash these dishes. I hate going to bed with dirty dishes left."

He looked at her absently, his lower lip drawn down. "Like James," she thought. "Aaron, you just like James. He couldn't forgive a thing." That would be a terrible thing to tell him. She heated water and poured it in the dishpan. The noise of its spattering seemed to sustain her. "Hand me that platter." She washed and dried and put away the dishes under a cloth. She stepped to the door and flung the water out. It froze as it hit the snow, sinking a little. Outside everything was quiet and dark. The strange wet smell of the snow mingled with the smell of the pork and the hominy. Hannah stood in the door, the pan glistening in her arms, the hairs of her arms rising up from the cold. "We don't have nothing," she announced softly to herself. "Not nothing." The tops of the pines jabbed at the grey sky. A clod of snow fell from the roof in front of her. "Except for Charlotte, all my girls is grown and married, pooched out from babies. The last sight I had of my boy was a big cloud of dust the hoss kicked up at me. 'I ain't sticking around here,' he said to me. *West*. He said he was making it *west*." Hannah frowned. She thought a moment to gain her bearings and turn west.

"How come you throwed that water out? You know I want it for the hawg slops."

She wearily turned, closing the door, and dried her hands. She ignored his last challenge. "I'm going on to bed," she said.

"Awright." He rose from the chair and banked the fire. Then he followed her down the hall that was an endless cold tunnel, a tunnel smelling of pork and polish and oil of camphor. They went along silently, almost furtively, like two old Indians. To the right of them rose the staircase, with its black balustrade. Nothing slept upstairs any more. In front of them, glimmering like the one-eyed Polyphemus, an oval glass was hung on the wall. Beneath it was James in his white skirts and leatherette boots. His apple-colored cheeks and fading eyes were uncomprehending as they passed below him.

The room was cold. Aaron Bloodworth liked to sleep in a cold room. And although enveloped by frigid air all night long, he kept a foot poked out from under the cover. Hannah was vaguely disturbed. She did not like Bloodworth's sulking spells. They had begun when the first hard weather had set in, not long after James's departure for the West. He had taken the best horse in the stable and he had gone without saying a word to his father or even asking his permission to go. Aaron Bloodworth had never been a sulking man. Now he sat and sulked like a bad child. It made her uneasy and she suffered bad dreams.

The two of them lay down without seeing each other, lay down and nestled into their accustomed places, hollowed out from years of such repose. She adjusted her pillow and began staring into the blackness. After a long, dark, undreaming space of time, Bloodworth spoke to her. "Something just made me think of Ed Darley. You recall Ed Darley?" He did not wait for her reply, but plunged on. "Ed Darley was younger than me. My birthday was in December and hisn was in July. He would have been maybe forty-seven years old this summer. I'm forty-eight. And now he's already dead. Makes me feel old, don't it you?" He broke off.

Hannah said nothing. She reached into the darkness with the arm of her mind and found *Edmund Darley, old-maidish bachelor, died of a galloping consumption, possessed of a mad craving for raw oysters in the final stages. Raw oysters! And no way to get them this far from the coast; died; washed and laid out by the women of the community (had he but known!); a nice funeral; buried at Rocky Run.*

After another long blindness, she was startled to hear Aaron break into laughter and slap his side of the bed. "I remember when we was younguns, one time at Rocky Run,

Ed Darley got down inside the well and hung by his two skinny hands!" Bloodworth sat up straight as a rod, his feet like hard chunks under the cover, scratching against her calves. "It was a home-coming and everybody else was inside. We dared Ed to do it. And he did! Hung there by his skinny bones, grinning at us. When I looked down at him, all I could see was the whites of his eyes. We helped him out, though. I wouldn't of never done that for love or nothing. God bless, no!" He paused for breath and Hannah interrupted.

"That sounds like Edmund Darley. Not one lick of common sense in him. And more trusting than a little nigger baby. It's a wonder he didn't meet his death sooner. But he never took no more chances like that. Never even got married or started no family. He died a horrible death, and in his own bed, too, with no one to ease him."

She waited for Aaron to interrupt her and defend Ed Darley. And when he didn't, she looked anxiously at his dark form lying beside her. He was not listening. He had deafened himself to her. What did she know of Darley's easement? Or whether or not his death had been horrible? Hannah knew nothing. Nothing. He was sure of her ignorance. He wondered how he could have been married to such a woman. In her youth, though, she had been fully fired, quick to flare. But each one of their redheaded younguns had taken some of it away from her. And James had taken the rest of it along with the best horse.

Bloodworth shrugged disgustedly as Hannah picked at the bedclothes around her chin. She didn't like the cold room and she used to rail at him about it, running a warmer stuffed with hot coals up and down her side until she thought she could survive the night. Now she just got in and pulled up the covers like her old shawl. He pontificated: *When I appear before the throne of God, I shall say to Him, "My wife, the one You gave to me called Hannah Bloodworth, is nothing but an old indigo-colored shawl and a pulled-up quilt."*

Then he took out a new weapon and explored her with it. "Folks do suffer. Even peaceable kinds of folks. Folks that don't take foolish chances. I suffered for Fred Elbert? You remember?"

He struck a mortal vein. The old familiar torment, repressed for a decade, returned to her. She grasped her covers and said harshly, "Remember! Me remember? Me who sat there day after day and watched him until the very day of his death! I can tell you the very day. March 7, 1832. Imagine that! March 7, 1832! And where was you, Aaron? You that don't take foolish chances. Grinding early wheat?" Hannah raised herself from the bed. The covers slipped from her shoulder. The neck of her nightdress hung open, and if there had been light in the room for him to see, Aaron Bloodworth would have seen her useless breasts hanging down like pale fingers over her ribs.

"How could I unremember it! In the morning, after breakfast, and you already gone. James was there." She closed her eyes in anguish, collecting the memory, choosing and rejecting among its terrible fragments. *James, you are so bad.* When she first held the newborn in her arms and gave him the breast, James became enraged. She felt those tiny hard fists beating against her neck and full breast. The chair shook under the small kicking boots. Her ears filled with the cries of her two sons. *Oh, James! How could you be so hateful!*

The tears were hot and ran down in the corners of her mouth and she tasted them. She opened her eyes again and saw that a few untidy stars had pimpled the grey sky and gave a faint glow to the snow on the windows. She had always been a tidy woman, scrubbing her house and her dishes and all her younguns until they gleamed. She never let her babies go wet. The neighbors laughed behind her back at her clothesline, which was always full. But the neighbors' babies wore dresses stiff from dried urine, stiff and yellow. Hannah yielded to her heavy anger.

"Listen to me!" She almost shrieked across the bed at him. "Listen, it was March and raining every day. That water pouring over the dam. Ain't no wheat in March, Aaron. You didn't have no business at the mill. You didn't have to go. But you did go!"

Hannah's voice cracked like a thin china plate. She grew softer. The flames of her died away to familiar ash, red, crumbling, grey-scaled. "Fred Elbert was choking with the croup. I'd done all I knowed. Fixed the kettle with a blanket over him. Hot poultices. I couldn't do no more. And James was there all the time, standing by the east window, spitting on his fingers and smearing the glass."

Hannah blinked at the stars. " 'James,' I said, soft and calmlike, so as not to alarm him none. 'James, come over here.' And when he come, I held Fred Elbert to me and I said, 'Will you please run down and fetch your pa? Please?' And he just stood there, his fingers digging in the side of the crib, digging and gouging so deep that when he taken them away, he left marks in the wood!"

Hannah lay down, abated. She rested a moment. Her old hot youth withdrew itself and she picked the bedclothes again. She continued quietly, "I held Fred Elbert and I started running. The rain soaked us to the skin. I looked back onct and seen James straggling behind, stomping in every mudhole he come to. The water sloshed high up on his leg. I didn't care any more. I didn't care if he got nasty, if he played in the mud and even shit on hisself. I run as hard as I could down to you." She turned her face toward Aaron Bloodworth. She nuzzled the cold slick pillow. "I had already ast you to send for Shanner that morning. And Fred Elbert was choked in less than an hour."

She settled into the pillow peacefully. She felt avenged by having blurted it all out this way. The stars began to brighten. They seemed to increase in size until they looked swollen with their light. She murmured from the first drownings of her sleep, "I should of quit when I had James." The words came from her lips thin, blurred, unrehearsed. "He was a bad youngun, too tough to choke. . . ." Hannah ground her teeth in sleep.

He had been still too long, allowing her to go on and on. "Now you spoke your piece, you listen awhile to me. I ain't forgot you stayed there. You bore your part!" But she was lost to any more. He lay stiff as a board.

In the night, the temperature warmed and toward morning the snow had begun to melt a little. It dripped off the eaves and fell deep into the drifts around the house, making long needle-pointed indentations. They rose and made breakfast. They had put away the night. And it did not occur to them again. Toward noon Doctor Tscharner appeared, driving a crude sledge. He told them the river was open and the ferry had crossed twice. His daughter, Elisabeth, would possibly come home by the last of March. He drove away. The iron runners of the sledge bit into the ice. The melting snow turned rapidly into grey slush.

24

He stood on the French coast in a dream. A strong north-easter was blowing and the cross tides ran in a frenzy. The cold grey sand blew against his legs and face, stinging, obliterating his eyeballs. He wandered about, suffering the wind to buffet and blast him. Sometimes he stumbled into the cold brine and he noticed, with alarm, that his feet were naked. They stood out terribly white and shiny, like the bellies of frogs, against the sea water.

A figure came toward him on the beach. He realized that it was Aaron Bloodworth. The man came closer and took his arm rudely and said, "You told me a lie, Shanner. You told me a bald-assed lie and you know it."

"About what?" His query was bounced by the harsh wind, dragged through the surf. It burst like suds on the beach. Bloodworth peered at him and his face was unpleasant. "About that railroad, Shanner." Then Bloodworth displayed all his excellent teeth in a broad grin like a satyr. He released Doctor Tscharner's arm. "I seen it myself and I tell you for a God's fact the Devil wouldn't of stood in front of that engine no moren a crabapple!"

The sound of dry coughing woke him. He opened his eyes, still seeing the teeth of Bloodworth and feeling the sting of the wind. He became aware of his place in bed and of the flickering in the fireplace. Cassandra knelt on the hearth. She had laid a fresh fire and seemed to be heating something in a cup. Her shoulders shook and she held one hand tightly over her mouth as if to choke down the spasms.

He lay quietly, watching. She was now twenty-seven years old and she was not as most women her age, dried up or bloated, round-shouldered, smelling of snuff, burdened. The hair spread thick and uneven over her shoulders. She often said to him, "I will cut my hair off and then I will gain. My hair takes everything." Now she was seized by a violent paroxysm. She sat back on her haunches. He got out of bed, speaking her name.

She glanced up, surprised and ashamed. "You don't need to get out of bed. I'm heating a little gargle of honey and vinegar. No need for you." The coughing overcame her. When she had finished, she sat with her hands clamped over her mouth, then took them down and resumed stirring in the cup.

He took the cup from her and made her swallow. He put his hands to her neck and rubbed it. He warmed a long woolen scarf and wrapped her neck. "Lie down," he directed, "A brandy toddy would be good for you now."

When he returned, she lay looking at him with amusement. "Why do you smile at me?" he asked.

"Oh," she said, waving her hand, "you are here, in your own warm bed. The night is cold out. And you are having to tend me. Does it seem fair?"

"It does not matter what is fair." He poured brandy into the still-warm cup and shook it to circulate the heat. She drank it for him and he sat on the side of the bed, gazing at the fire. After a while, he began to speak.

"I was dreaming just now, before I wakened. I dreamed of the sea. And of myself. You have never seen the sea." The logs in the fire shifted and he glanced around at her. "It is hysterical. Wild and shattering, a terrible, beautiful thing." He flushed as pinkly as if he himself were inflamed with a quinsy.

"We crossed the sea. Kaethe and I." It was the first he had ever spoken her name to Cassandra's ear. She felt jealous in a secret and inarticulate way. He sounded wistful as he said it and that distressed her.

"I went about on deck. The sight of the sea both repelled and drew me. I did not understand it, but I wanted to know all of it, its moods, its horrors, its condescending tolerance of my feeble ship." He spoke with a childish eagerness. "There are dolphin in the sea. They follow a ship, playing and leaping in the wake of it." His eyes beseeched her for an approval, then he went on. "There in the midst of the sea, I found something I had lost for a great time." He began to drink from the brandy bottle. "And my wife, Kaethe, died without knowing it."

Cassandra's distress mounted as he said the name again. She could make no sound. He kept on talking to her. He overwhelmed her with his unfamiliar talk, too much talk.

"It is sometimes in dim, half-alive moments between sleeping and waking that I can recapture something of that effect." He rubbed his thumb around the bottle neck. "The view at Jutta is of a valley. There is the Moselle River. It flows from the Vosges in France, almost three hundred miles, to the Rhine. The soil is very good. My list of troubles was short there. I was the eldest son, on whom all their hopes rested. My father thrust music into my hands. It was his livelihood and I did not argue, but music could never flourish within me or because of me. I was not the prodigy he wanted." He stopped. He seemed to reach about in the reddish shadows of the room, clutching at his words, which spilled forth like fish, undisciplined.

"Cassandra, can you imagine the distance between here, between this place and the sea? Then the terrible expanse of that water-world, and when at last it comes to an end, the enormous stretch of coast and high mountains that one must traverse to reach my homeland?"

She whispered, "Yes," and wrinkled her forehead. She felt she was locked tightly in a strange new nightmare, a dream of Doctor Tscharner's splitting open and leaking out his life juices. She did not want to see his juices. They were too unfamiliar. And it was all highly questionable. But she nodded, unable to restrain herself, and he rushed on, his words flooding over her like flames over a resinous chunk of lightwood.

"But I have neglected my original intention of telling you the strange effect the sea cast over me. I had what you may call visions as a child. Once I saw a lion walk into my room at Jutta. He had a yellow mane and he opened his mouth to roar and his teeth were terrifying." He smiled. "I did not tell my mother. It would have been impossible. And another time I saw myself dead. I saw exactly how it would be. I lay in a long black coffin and my head rested on a small pillow fringed with silk. The coffin smelled like the boot blacking I had to use. I saw thumbprints the pallbearers had left on the lid."

Cassandra rustled her feet under the sheet and it startled him. He smiled again and lay across the bed, his head resting on her hip. "It was then that I decided I would die away from home, in some disaster. A war or an earthquake. Anything to avoid that vulgar boot blacking." An unusual awe crept into his voice and he whispered, "I would like to drop into the sea."

"No," Cassandra interrupted. Her breathing was rapid and her eyes were shiny with her infection. "No," she repeated. She wanted to strike it all down. Her tonsils hurt as she protested, "I don't understand. I mean perhaps I do understand about your visions and about the sea. But I don't about the other you said, dropping into the sea and drowning. Have you ever seen a drowned man?" She coughed and pounded at her throat under the thick scarf.

"One spring the river was high and the eddy was on the Weymouth side. I found a drowned man, I mean a dead man. I'm not sure that he was really drowned. Pa sent for the coroner from Wharftown, and when he turned the man over, his eyeballs fell out and then his mouth turned wrong side and all of it floated away." The firelight danced before her fevered eyes. "You know, the coroner said it was death by drowning. But why didn't he come ashore in Weymouth? The eddy was on Weymouth side. He should have come ashore there."

She touched his arm. "You don't want to lie in the water dead." He gazed at her, fascinated by her, by her sickness, her distress, her parable. "They brought a pine box, not even a real coffin, and put him inside it. It had big cracks and green flies swarmed in and out and the smell of him was awful." She shook her head at him. "Maybe you're just testing me. You never have been a fearing man. I don't mean you aren't a good man. Oh, I don't really mean anything." She swallowed with a dreadful choking feeling.

Doctor Tscharner replied sensibly, acknowledging the facts, "Your plain ignorance is a cure."

She reached out and struck him across the face. "Don't you call me ignorant. I'm not all that ignorant. I guess you've felt put out having me for a wife these years. But I'm more than she was. You know I am." Cassandra began to weep hoarsely.

He was shocked. His skin pulsated where she had struck him. And she had said the truth. The sentences glimmered in his brain. He leaned over her. "Cassandra, I have been unkind. I have burdened you."

"No! No!" She brushed his hands away and glared at him. "I want to be burdened. Please burden me!"

He was astounded. He was pleased. He kissed her and

her lips were febrile. "I have seen death, too, Cassandra, and smelled putrefaction. I know that it takes away all that men try to become. But the fact that you and I can comprehend such thoughts is more significant than perhaps the sea, which has no mind and comprehends nothing." He concluded. And she listened to the reverberation of his voice, which came, strangely, from inside his shoulder. She was warm. She shut her eyes again.

The new moon, sharp as a white sickle, hung in the sky. Doctor Tscharner noticed it and pointed at the window. Cassandra nodded. Her throat throbbed and the pulse beat in her temple. *Significant. Significant.*

25

The first martins appeared. Whippoorwills were heard. The snow melted and the river cleared and was strong. Doctor Tscharner directed the planting of an early garden. His Negroes laid small drills to receive the seeds. And he raised a second vineyard on the side of Apion Mountain. Over a hundred varieties came to him by post from the Luxembourg in Paris. Some were dead, dried up, yellow as chicken feet. But others still lived and they pleased him. Ishmael charred the ends of posts to resist decay from the wet earth. And Clegg dug holes for them. The arbors were made ready and the delicate vines were placed. Suddenly it

Then the laugh was drawn out, too. It was a quiet, apologetic laugh, polite and colored like the dripping, diminishing rain outside. "I had a dainty foot in the dance. I danced with my young new husband, Hartwell Peck, who didn't have any more sense than I did. Both of us parrots in cages. Pretty birds decked out for the big kill."

She gestured with the peacock feather. "Here, take it, take it. I should keep dried cattails in my vases. Not this dried-up and frivolous tailpiece." She held it out to him and added wryly, "Do not worry. I can pay for your visit in cash, too. I only want this thing to go out with you."

Doctor Tscharner turned it around in the new light that came from the window. It was a fragile thing, a long hollow shaft, its fringes faded. A faint green iridescence caught in the light, strained and indefinite. He chuckled and asked her, "What should I do with this?"

"Take it to your daughter. I've heard you have a pretty one. Ah, but you aren't the sort to make presents. So stick it in a pot in the corner. Swat flies with it." She shook her head, rubbing at her chest. "I should have swatted Hartwell Peck. But that is all gone and behind me. Now I lie down to sleep and I stifle. I am weak and my heart palpitates."

She looked at him with a vague sidelong glance and he saw that her eyes were extremely blue and clear against the redness of their rims. It startled him and he said brusquely to gain his composure, "Avoid late suppers, madam, and employ the habit of tonic at bedtime. And, if you can, do not sleep on your back at all."

He bade her farewell and went out in the damp glittering air. Drops of water fell on his head from the eaves and they felt startlingly cold. He saw her face at the window as he rode past and the blue eyes were vacant. She held a hand to her chest.

He rode through the wet forest feeling strangely discontented, yet calmed down by his visit with the old woman. She seemed to have cast an anodyne across his impatience. And at the bottom of it, he was restless that it might soon wear off and the impatience return stronger than before. He distracted himself. He thought of his son, Neil, who was eleven years old and healthy. He showed every indication of a fine intelligence and Doctor Tscharner reminded himself to arrange a passage to Europe for this son. This son would receive the best education. This son would return to make a mark.

He began to feel cheerful. The sudden clearing of the rain elated him. The trees had turned green earlier this spring because of the heavy rain. Arbutus showed in the open places of the woods. When he returned home, a letter had been brought by the postboy. It came from Lieschen. She was to be expected the following week for an Easter holiday. He read it with satisfaction and he realized for the first time that he would be glad to see her again. He thought, too, of the old woman's peacock feather. But when he took it from under his cape, it was broken and the thin feathers had frayed into an ugly mess. He cast it in the fire. The fine feather, fine as hair, burned in a pouf and the bone melted. Doctor Tscharner sat down and wrote in his log:

Easter, the Christian festival of resurrection, is at hand. To us it is no more than the return of the spring. To the ancients it was the first full moon after the vernal equinox.

216

The days are yet cool. No frost. Clearing skies. River full. Lieschen returns to us.

She looked sallow. He saw that the bone of her chin had become prominent and stuck out over her high collar. She had not grown. Her eyes pierced him and held him, on a long pin. "Elisabeth." He could not help the smile that went to his face on beholding her, on comprehending the image of her. He had brought the best carriage across the river, leaving his wife and son on Apion. It was as he wished: he alone to bring her back. Now her eyes kept piercing him, holding him at a distance, and his good humor suffered. "Hello, Doctor Tscharner," she said. Her yellow hair was tied back under a net.

He put the trunk into the carriage and helped her. Nodding to the people, his patients, his debtors, Doctor Tscharner drove off with his daughter. She did not pay any attention to the passing scene, and when they reached the ferry, she continued to reply to his questions with dull words.

Midstream, she glanced over the high rushing water. The cables over them shrieked. The ferryman stood on the Y-shaped runway looking at her. It was Jonah Keith. His sprawling house had a new ell tacked on behind. The raw wood shone yellow against the grey boards of the old part. There was a crowd of dirty children playing in the yard. A little one in skirts—she could not tell if it was a girl or a boy—swung on the broken gate. As the carriage rolled off the ferry and passed, the child opened its mouth to grin. Lieschen saw that its teeth were blackened and snaggled.

They arrived in time for supper. She gave presents to

Neil and to Cassandra. They ate and went to bed. She lay in her bed again and felt the familiar rustlings of the sheets and the squeaking of the headboard against the wall. She saw that she was home and that it had been hard to exchange one environment for another and not lose her identity. She did not feel familiar at the school. And now that she had left the school and the girls with their pretty blurred faces, she no longer felt familiar in her own bed.

The pretty faces of the girls blurred into one huge blur the color of weak tea. They did not excel, as she did, at mathematics or French. They lay down at night and breathed asthmatically, their bodies pink and unexplored. The months had passed. And she was angry. She didn't know why. When the snow came to the city, she went out and plunged through the deepest drifts, plucking ice off the tree branches and sucking at it. The taste of the ice had been very dull. In March, in the same city, the trees were swelling. The ground was soft and well watered. But the girls with their pretty, dull, blurred faces and their pretty, blurred, uncleft bodies had not noticed any change. It made her desperately angry.

She was now back on Apion. The sky was heavy-colored, too blue. And her youth appeared to be paralyzed, ill-fed, and thirsty.

26

"You are still here." She declared the fact before him bluntly.

"Yes." He smiled. His skin seemed more freckled than before and his hair was white as dust, faded-looking. The sight of him did not appeal to her, and when he put his hand boldly, assumingly, over hers, she was very annoyed and drew her own away.

"I saw Jonah when I crossed with my father. He has a crowd of children." She was curious in spite of her annoyance. And she asked him bluntly, "Are you part of his crowd, too?"

He shrugged. "I have no use for that river, for hauling people over it all day and night. I make my own way, Lizzie."

"But you are still *here*. In Larkin County." She challenged him. "I cannot see why you are still in a place like this."

They sat on Doctor Tscharner's sofa. It was made of black horsehair, very slick, and had been given to him by a patient as payment for the removal of a terrible tumor. Cassandra sat opposite the sofa, on a cane-bottomed chair. They paid her no mind. There was nothing she could do to them anyway.

"I thought of going long ago. You thought of it. You want to go like I do. I think I'm ready, Lizzie. And I think maybe you want to be made ready yourself. To go with me, I mean." He pressed her hand and she felt how hard and rough were his calluses. And he had stopped smiling at her. He returned her own blunt paralyzing stare and Lieschen recoiled in horror. She pulled her hand away again and frowned at him and retorted, "You waited? Why would I go? Why would I even want to be made ready?"

He did not think twice over it. He kept his long freezing stare that was a deadly mimic of her own. Then he relented and smiled again and said assuredly, aiming at the target she had set on herself, "Because. Because Ohio's biggern here."

That pleased her. And the truth of it was alarmingly simple. But she could not allow him to win so easily. "I do not love you at all," she declared.

"That will not matter to me now. Nor to you either, Lizzie. Not right now."

Cassandra burst upon them furiously. "You neither one knows what matters! How can you know? You've both got beds. You've got something to eat. There's nobody that's laid a stick to you. How can you leave these things? How can you just go off and leave all that?"

Leischen did not make a reply. Her eyes absorbed the room she sat in: Doctor Tscharner's horsehair sofa, the ticking of the grandfather clock in the next room, the face of Cassandra, swollen with apprehension and anger. She heard soft steps across the floor over her head. Neil, she knew it was, in the loft, listening. She put her fingers defiantly back into Boone's hand and the touch of the calluses reminded her of the cylinder in the music box. The music box, she had discovered, had begun to throw back a tinny echo as uncomfortable as the whanging of a jew's-harp.

Somehow, the roughness of the calluses helped to decide her. She dressed her face and said to him, without emotional strain, "You are right. I will go."

"No." Cassandra sprang from the cane chair and took Lieschen by her arm. She was not an emotional woman herself and the years with Doctor Tscharner had not seen much weeping. But now she began to weep terribly. The feeling was degrading to her. But she passed over her feeling, trying to reach for the girl that was Doctor Tscharner's girl. "Please, you think it's something you can do. And you are quite right. But please don't do it. I know you're not contented. I can feel it all over you and I have been feeling it ever since I first came here. It's awful. It's hurtful. I know. But it won't last you, Lieschen. Boone might last you. He might last and last until both of you are

221

so sick you can't stand it any more. Then where will you be?"

Cassandra did not like what she was doing, the tears that streaked her face; the sound of her pleading disgusted her. But she knew no other way to do it. She swallowed heavily. "You should have seen yourself sitting in that pony cart, boots and stockings all the way up to your straddle, petticoats, skirts, and a gold locket around your neck that you didn't ever do anything but chew on. I never had a petticoat, I mean a real one all my own, until I came here and he gave it to me. I never sat in a pony cart. And I never had any decorations, anything made out of real gold." She held out her hands to the girl. "I don't have any now. Do you see any on me?"

She sat down in the cane chair. Her cheeks glistened, but the weeping had gone out of her. She became what she had always been, a hard strange mother-girl who believed in no more than Doctor Tscharner and sometimes in herself. Her remorse was fading. Lieschen would do as she wished. It made no difference what she, Cassandra, had said to her. But she yet could not allow her to go away hating him this way, in this terrible amount. She made one more half-hearted attempt to retrieve Lieschen for him.

"I don't grudge you for those petticoats and things. I never have. I came here and you were a little thing and I saw you were all he had and he was all you had. But neither of you really had each other, really wanted each other. He was always busy. And what you did, children's stuff, was nothing that he'd care for. Oh, it was bad. It was wrong. And I didn't do not one solitary thing but just look at it." She put her head in her hands, rocking forward on her knees like an old woman. Her voice changed. She took on the dull peasant speech she had once thrown off. "Get on, now. I ain't trucking no more with you, either one of you. And you still don't know damned nothing."

Boone waited. Lieschen got up and put out her hand to touch Cassandra. "I know the truth," she whispered with hard conviction, "I do know."

Doctor Tscharner wanted to talk to Lieschen. He wanted to tell her of the peacock feather and the old woman and the uncanny familiarity she had aroused. Suddenly all the old gates and dikes were opened and he wanted to show this new Lieschen, who was, of course, the same Lieschen. He wanted to show her the vineyards were surviving. They were like her, new strains, rare breeds, transplanted to an alien soil, and they were surviving.

But the animal dailiness of life thwarted him. He was called to all sorts of absurdities—toothache, delivery, malignancy. He had to make himself ready and ride off unrequited. But he promised himself it would be done when he came back.

And when he came back, it was dark. He went straight to bed without supper and without noticing the absence of his child Lieschen.

The next morning Cassandra told him. He sat like a stone, a lump of flint; the light in his eyes dazzled her. His son, Neil, was still at table eating porridge. Doctor Tscharner looked at the brown sugar slowly dissolving in warm milk. He followed the spoon as it dug into the porridge, moved through space, and went into Neil's mouth. He did not see

Neil at all. He only heard Cassandra speaking the words. He waited patiently until she had finished. His comment was a terrible one to her. "Was she pregnant?"

"Does it make any difference?" Cassandra studied his face and saw there was no possible answer, neither to his question, nor to hers. She vowed she would never plead for anything from him again.

Doctor Tscharner ate his breakfast. And after eating, he went to the surgery and attended his patients of the day. A boy was brought by his mother. He had proud flesh growing on the back of his hand. The ulcer was raw and red granulations had spread. The mother suffered from a severe catarrh and had a red peeling nose which she nervously wiped and stuffed with her handkerchief. Doctor Tscharner cleaned the boy's sore with limewater. He covered the place with a soft bandage.

For the woman, he recommended breathing over a pan of hot water. "You can take a pinch of snuff mixed with red pepper if the stuffiness persists." He gave her tallow to rub on her nose. She put it in her apron, all the while rubbing at the raw nose. "I guess you get tired of seeing nothing but sickness and misery, Doctor," she remarked. Then she grinned. "But you couldn't make no living if it won't for sick folks!" A drop of mucus glistened and slid down her upper lip. She dabbed at it and took the boy's arm.

"On the contrary," said Doctor Tscharner pitilessly, "there's nothing I desire more than good health." He shut the door rudely in her face and turned to his other bad ones. The day passed in a long gloomy menagerie: proud flesh, catarrh, worms, scald head.

"Wash the child's head," he commanded. The smell was

offensive and her scalp was covered with tiny white scabs. "Then apply ointment made from pride of China and tobacco juice."

The girl stared at him. "You mean chiney berries that grows on chiney trees?"

He nodded impatiently.

"They's poison. Ise seen hawgs fall over and die, their legs stiffern posts in a few minutes, after eating them chiney berries! I ain't greasing this youngun with no chiney berries."

Doctor Tscharner narrowed his eyes. He crashed his hand on the table. "If you do not cure this child as I have told you, then I will take my razor and shave her head until she is bald!"

"I'll do it! I'll do it!" affirmed the girl, clutching up the child. "Ifen chiney berries is what you say is best, I'll put chiney berries on her haid. Thanky, Doctor, thanky." She backed out the door. The child scratched at her scalp and the white scabs broke under her sharp little nails. She sniffed them like a cat. Doctor Tscharner crashed his hand on the table.

"Scum!" he shouted in his brain. "Dregs!"

27

Neil liked the plant shed. Its many panes of glass cheered him. Even in deepest winter, he felt the plant shed was a warm place. The shining bubbly glass warmed him. The panes were thin as fingernails. The slightest thump would crack them. He breathed on the glass. The twin spots spread into one and evaporated.

A. D. carefully dislodged the soil around the roots of the orange tree. He lifted it out, wincing as the long green spikes touched his skin. "Hold thisun," he said to Neil. The tree was large as the boy. He grasped it with both hands and shivered at the spikes. "This one's mine," he murmured into its leaves, smelling it, inhaling deeply.

A. D. held the roots in his lap and began tediously cutting away all those too long. The task made him nervous. His fingers were agile, cautious and explorative. But he trembled and was tense and irritable. A. D. feared he might injure the taproot and cause the tree's death and bring about the displeasure of Doctor Tscharner. He jumped when Neil asked, "We going to do Lieschen's, too?"

A. D. released his breath in a long hiss, wiped his hands, and laid the snippers on the ground. The floor of the plant shed was hard-packed dirt spread over with pine straw. "I reckon," he replied. "Why not?"

"I don't know." Neil tossed it off. His question was silly. Lieschen's tree was better than his. Even now, without being trimmed properly, it had put forth new buds. They were raised up all over it in little kernels.

He gazed at it admiringly. Lieschen had always supervised the reboxing of her orange tree, making sure A. D. placed it properly and added enough charcoal to the compost. She flew into a rage if the tree leaned in any direction. She wanted it perfectly straight, with all the leaves wiped clean. She never paid attention to any of the growing things on Apion Mountain. But this tree in the plant shed she wanted to be well kept. It had never borne any fruit. None of the tropical trees had borne fruit. But they continued to live and put out new buds each year.

A. D. set the orange tree squarely in the box and began filling in the fresh soil. Neil mixed charcoal and compost. They packed it firmly. They reboxed Lieschen's tree and also the lemon tree. And when this was done, Neil left, smelling of compost, perspiring heavily from the heat of the shed, and began to walk.

He disappeared in the woods, thinking about Lieschen, thinking so hard his head hurt. She had come back to Apion. She had not quarreled with anyone. And in the end, she had gone off Apion with Boone Keith, the son of the old ferryman, his old dead grandfather.

Neil stopped and stood stupefied, realizing that Boone Keith, whose face was covered with freckles, whose hands were hard with calluses, and whose hair stood up like dusty wheat in a field, this Boone Keith was his uncle, as was Jonah, the loudmouth on the river. The knowledge split him open. Pheny had said to him, once when he was little and had kicked her, "You got Keith blood in you, boy." It had never seemed to him that he had Keith blood. Or that he had Tscharner blood. His name was Neil and the name of his blood was Neil. He became enraged and kicked the ground, sending up showers of dirt and leaves. They were not his uncles. Never. Cassandra Keith had been the receptacle of his gestation, the vehicle of his birth, but she was no kin to him. She belonged entirely to the man Tscharner.

And what of Lieschen, the girl who was part his? Part his sister. When she went off Apion, she had paused at the bottom and waited for him to catch up. "Lieschen!" he had blurted. The March sun falling through pale new leaves dappled her skin green. Even her black rebellious eyes had assumed a weird greenish hue, astounding him. "Lieschen," he repeated. She held the music box under her arm. "Lieschen," he said for the third time, looking at all of her, "where are you going?"

She studied him carefully. Then, brushing at the dust on her skirt, she replied, "It doesn't matter to you." She shifted the music box and followed Boone Keith.

"Wait. Oh, Lieschen, let me go." He trotted beside them. She kept on walking and said, "No. Go away." Boone Keith kept moving steadily down the road, his shoulders straight, with no slump in his spine.

"But, Lieschen!" He ran around to face her, standing in front of her so she had to stop. "But, why not?" He felt dizzy, sick at his stomach.

She did not answer him, merely changed the music box from one arm to the other, then walked around him and kept going.

Then he had run after her, grabbed the music box from under her arm and hurled it to the ground. The wooden box splintered on the stones and the little metal cylinder rolled out. She looked at it and saw it was ruined. But she said nothing and kept walking after Boone.

Lieschen had disappeared. Neil walked on in the woods, kicking and raging at himself. He found the river. It dashed muddy spray against the rocks at his feet. The day was fair and he saw Weymouth clearly and could distinguish the kinds of trees growing on that side—pine, oak, dark cedar. He sat down. At once, dampness seeped through his pants and made him cold. Birds were shrieking in the trees. A squirrel appeared on a branch, grey and indistinct, his tail a murky cloud. Neil stared at the rushing water and forced an evolution through his brain. The hateful form of Lieschen fluttered by him, was torn in the water, and her last shreds hung from the thorns like yellow foam.

28

They were healed of Lieschen, stitched over, smeared with tallow. But the people would not allow her to be rubbed into obscurity. She had a lasting effect. And Aaron Bloodworth hated her gossip.

His customers came to the mill with June wheat. They rested on his porch, choked with dust, the sweat trickling down their necks. Their gossip had not worn off yet. Everyone wanted to own a piece of Doctor Tscharner. Their tongues clacked over the tale until it became a parable and a litany. *The clefts in the rock. The little foxes that spoil*

*the vine. And when it was morning, the east wind brought
the locusts.*

His vines, the green things that flourished and brought
forth, increased all over his mountain. Doctor Tscharner
had come among the people to cure them by the laying on
of his long lean hands, by purging with roots and bark, by
the letting of their blood under a steel edge. He had not
been friendly. He had not been a talkative sort. He appeared out of the wilderness with his black horse. And the
wilderness was more familiar than his face. He brought
laudanum drops to obliterate their pain, camomile flowers
to clear their bowels, sugar of lead, extract of belladonna,
pisswort, hart's-tongue, the pride of China. His materia
medica dazzled their ears and eyes and tongue. But the
afflictions he named upon them—swine pox, *tic doulou-
reux*, pleurisy, scirrhus—these afflictions named and ex-
pounded lifted them into a new state of grace, gave them a
prominence, brought down upon them mercies. He rode for
miles through the forest to treat their fevers and curse the
midwives for their filth. He crossed the river and he spent
the night.

He had brought one wife, a thin blonde wife, across the
big water. She had not spoken their language. They rarely
saw her. Some reported she suffered from fits, was touched,
though none could be certain. And she mysteriously died
and was buried in the forest behind his house. He was then
left with the child that was blond like the wife, but who had
his own piercing eyes. And she was never seen off Apion
Mountain.

They clacked over the tale tirelessly. Hannah Bloodworth joined them. Her wonderment and her great relish annoyed her husband. "Why did he stay here?" she kept asking. "I ast him onct."

"What'd he say?" encouraged a listener on the porch.

Hannah shook her head in desperation. "He didn't say nothing. Just looked at me like I was a fool." A gleam came to her eyes. "But then I plainly told him that child of hisn was a borned citizen, a natural-borned citizen." She swelled with self-righteousness.

"La." They wagged their heads. "And now that gal's run off with Boone Keith. Looks like he'd of lit out after 'em."

"Barsh." Bloodworth glared at them. "That ain't his way. His ways ain't yourn. Barsh!"

The talk wound around and grated like the burrstones and piled up into sacks. Each man came with his wheat and he flailed the story of Doctor Tscharner as he had flailed the grain, crudely, by hand, with a swingle bar.

Aaron Bloodworth's married children came to visit him in the evening. The land resounded with insects, thousands of insects and birds, and the close scurrying of animals. The grandchildren clustered around their mothers. Yellow light fell on them from Hannah's kerosene lamp. Bloodworth looked at each of them in the unreal yellow light and they struck him as being unreal creatures, things that did not bear his lineage. Some of them had red hair, the hair that had belonged to Hannah and James, to the girl called Mary June. There was not one of them that had his perfect teeth. His daughters dipped snuff and that disgusted him.

He poked his stick at the children and they moved back, flying up and lighting down again like a swarm of insects.

These things did not have his name. His name had gone west with James. It had choked to death and decayed in the ground with Fred Elbert. Bloodworth looked down at his stick. He was not really an old man yet. His hair fell out in patches, but he was not really old or in need of the stick. But he liked the stick. He liked to have it in his hands always. The knob was carved in the head of an animal, a horse, with an ugly Roman nose more like a mule's.

"I heard tell that Keith gal was in a family way when he married her," one of his daughters spoke from the yellow circles. "What do you know about that, Pa?" They all looked at him and waited to hear what he would say.

"I don't know nothing," he said fiercely.

"Pshaw," sneered the daughter's husband, a nameless lump of a man who had married her and begot children on her that Doctor Tscharner had had to bring out of her.

Bloodworth beat on the floor with his stick. "What are you snorting at? Most folks is, ain't they? You got gals yourself. Don't throw no stones. You might get hit."

A rumble of thunder concluded their talk. The daughter of Aaron Bloodworth and her sisters gathered their children and left him. He had done nothing to change their minds about Doctor Tscharner. He went to bed and slept with his foot hanging out and the mule-knob stick on the floor beside. A few raindrops fell into the dust and thunder sounded irregularly, accompanied by streaks of lightning, all night. But the storm did not come.

It held off for another month. The earth had sucked all the water of the melted snow. The earth had been broken open, plowed, and seeded. Plants sprouted, grew to about two inches, then wilted in the sun, were cut off by worms. The earth was broken again, plowed and crumbled, reseeded. But no rain fell and no clouds assembled. The thunder kept apart.

In July, the thunderhead suddenly appeared high in the sky. Electricity flared through the valley and the mountain grew dark. One half of the sky still shone brilliantly blue and the trees glittered with a green illumination. The other half was blackened by the approaching thunderhead. Then everything turned black.

Lightning jerked across the sky from cloud to cloud and from cloud to earth. Lumps of hail began to beat on the trees, peppering the shingles of the people's houses, and also the surface of the river. The terrifying boom of the thunder expanded over Apion Mountain and down the long valley. It seemed to cast down stones, so intensely did it boom and roar and crash. The people were thunderstruck, deafened by it as from the firing of great cannon on a war field. They ran to shelter, pulling their frightened animals with them, snatching up the chickens.

Sheets of rain lashed down. They blew from all directions and they exploded in smells of sulphur from the lightning. And behind the rain and the terrible electricity, the winds gathered their force.

Piles of hail lay on the road and filled up the new-plowed furrows. Lumps the size of black walnuts beat the green corn to tatters. The cane was bent over.

The winds began to move. They circulated in violent currents, ripping young trees from the earth, sweeping back the grass, scattering the hard bullet hail. The storm had come and was hateful.

‡

Earlier, in the morning, Doctor Tscharner was splitting pine. The labor refreshed him. The lifting of the ax and the cleaving of wood purged him of all impurities. He lifted the ax and in a terrible skull-cracking strike sank in it the block up to the helve. He relished each strike he made upon the wood. The wood cracked open and the resin came out colored gold. He swung and swung until his muscles ached and he had to stop, leaving the ax deep in the block, the handle warm from his hands.

He noticed the thick mass of clouds piling in the sky. The breezes swept over him and raised the hair from his scalp. He was occupied, distracted. He had to make a ride.

While at the house of his patient, the sky turned very dark and the people set candles in dishes on the table near him. They looked fearfully at the approaching clouds, the burst of the lightning. They were nervous. "I hate this house under pine woods," said one, an old man with palsy. "Lightning loves to strike a pine."

"I seen lightning strike onct," contributed another, a younger one, whose wife was big with child. "It struck a youngun standing under a big oak tree. It made little bitty holes in the dust, all around him in a circle. And he was burnt black. And me, I was standing on the porch, at least five foot away, and it knocked me plumb down. I didn't feel right in my head for a week."

Doctor Tscharner finished with his patient and made to leave. They warned him not to go out. They asked him to stay until the storm had gone. He considered the sky. It did not look alarming to him. He left, feeling sure that he could reach Apion before the rain fell. He had not gone a fourth of the way when the sky opened over his head.

The rain fell in such torrents, tearing leaves from trees, that Doctor Tscharner could not find his way. Everything drowned in a grey gush of water illuminated at points by the cracking light. Hailstones pelted him, causing the horse to jerk. The winds surrounded them and drove them backward to the river, where the bank was crumbling under the slaughtering rain. And in a great confusion, the horse descended into the water, submerging Doctor Tscharner beneath him.

The black horse was carried swiftly downstream. He neighed dolorously, his eyeballs white and slick as eggs. The sky cast down stones. Electricity sprang through the air and lit up the woods as bright as noon. Branches fell and whole thickets of birch and willow were torn away.

The winds sped up the side of Apion Mountain and blew down all the trees until it was naked and the red roots of the trees were left sticking up in the rain. Glassy balls of rain pulsated over the face of the river as regularly as veins in a fontanel. The hollow hundred-year trees fell into the river with great noises.

AN EPILOGUE:
NAKED MOUNTAIN

The cyclone exhausted itself in the night. When it was over, the people could not truly believe they had been delivered. Boards had been lifted off and driven horizontally against the houses, sometimes bursting through the windows. Horses and cattle had bolted from the stables and been lost in the downpour. Drowned chickens floated in the wide green-colored pools that filled all the barnyards.

The ferryman's house had been destroyed, pieces of it blown into the river, some of it blown across the river into Weymouth. His boat was gone; the dock shattered.

The mill of Aaron Bloodworth was wrecked like a

wooden toy. And the water poured over the dam in a heavy glassen roll, so heavy that the dam could not be seen beneath it and it appeared as a steady spilling, thick as boiling molasses.

Wells and cisterns, the caves and holes of the mountain were filled with water and the swollen river reverberated over the Falls. The biggest trees that had withstood the winds were bent and broken into craggy shapes as though some giant from the mountain had pulled them over and sat on them. And the mountain itself was naked.

The people came out and stood in the yellow mists that steamed from the wetness. They went about like sleepwalkers, stunned, deafened. Then they hallooed across the valley to one another. The slave people of Doctor Tscharner, who had come to the house during the storm and begged to be let in, stood around his wife and wondered at his absence. Every pane in the plant shed was broken. Cassandra looked down the road that was glutted with leaves and bright water and she felt she had just come from finishing a hard, long task.

The victims of the wind began to gather. Those with crushed hips and broken jaws. Those with severely palpitating hearts. They arrived slowly, their mules laboring over the debris in his yard.